Remote Man

Blurb
Internet
Planet
Reptile
Adventure
Huma
Bear
Chat
Frying pan

OK

Published by
Dell Yearling
an imprint of
Random House Children's Books
a division of Random House, Inc.
New York

Visit us on the Web! www.randomhouse.com/kids

Educators and librarians, for a variety of teaching tools, visit us at
www.randomhouse.com/teachers

ISBN: 0-440-41901-8

Reprinted by arrangement with Alfred A. Knopf

Printed in the United States of America

January 2004

10 9 8 7 6 5 4 3 2 1

OPM

Elizabeth Honey

ReMOTE MAN

A Dell Yearling Book

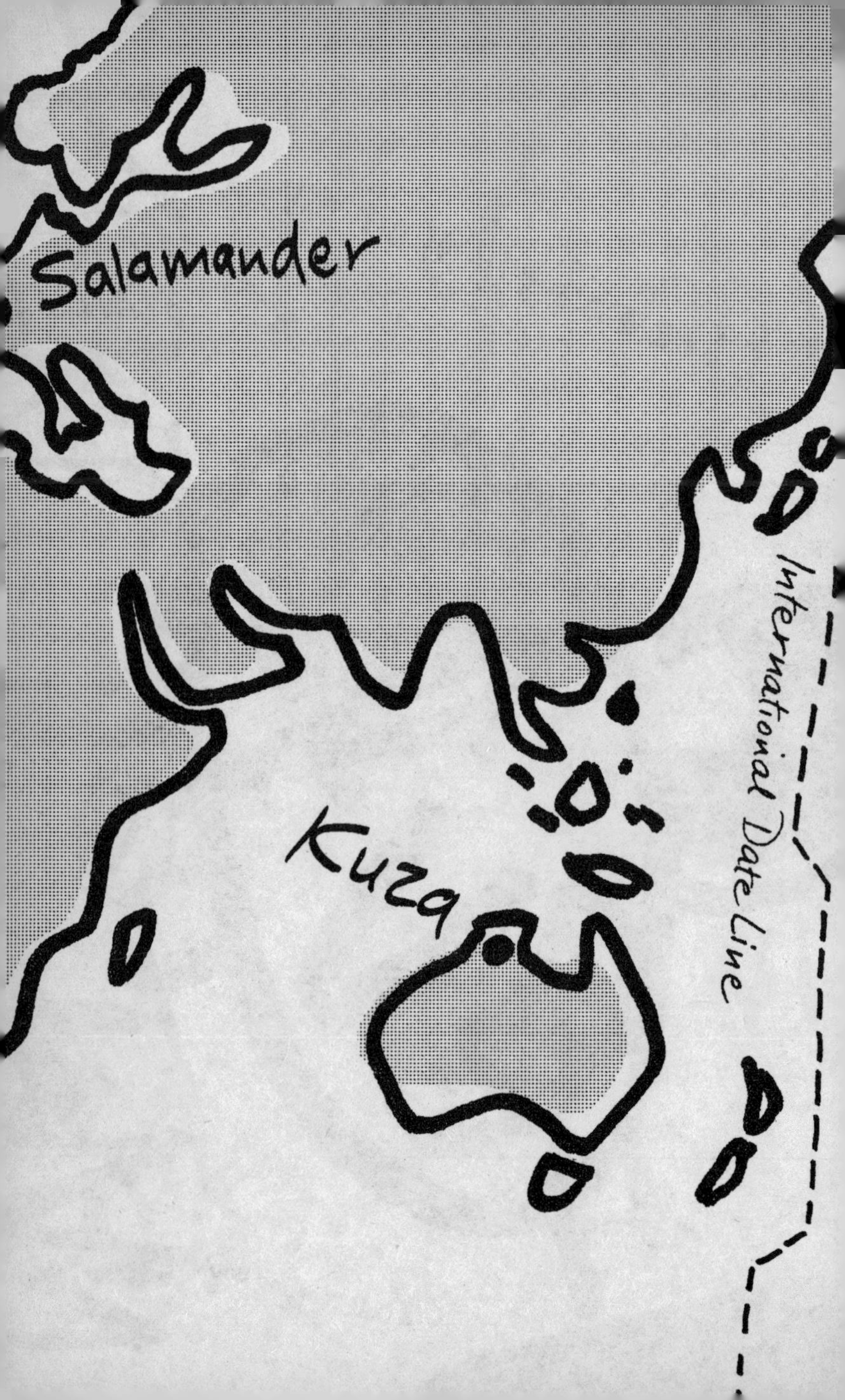

Salamander
Kuza
International Date Line

Remote Man
Rocky•

•Ja

Who?

Where?

CONTENTS

for Andrew

Seriously Weird

Has my McLaren F1 been delivered? Nope. Didn't think so.

Ned dumped his schoolbag by the door and stubbed off his old Nikes. Then he grabbed the remote, took a short run, and in one fluid movement crashed back onto the couch as he flicked on the TV.

"...get outta here. It's headed straight for us. We..."

"The bat in Patagonia..."

"Feeling hungry?"

"...you don't understand. He killed my brother. I've..."

An hour later, Ned was still watching aimlessly, prowling the channels. He watched a car chase to the ads, flicked to an air show, a jealous feud and back to the drama in the stolen car. He looked at the kitchen clock. Half past six.

Any minute now, he thought.

The phone rang.

Yep, she's been kidnapped again!

"Janet and Ned aren't home right now. Please leave a message." Beep.

"Hello, Ned." She knew he was there. Her voice was flat. "Take the pie out of the freezer and put it in the oven, please. I'll be home around eight." Click.

They force her to talk to prove she's alive.

Ten minutes passed. Then he heard the steady growl of the fax. He stood up and stretched. He was a lanky kid, not tall yet, but his loose limbs and big feet made you think of a puppy with large paws. He walked into his mother's study and ripped off the fax.

Could have guessed. Bet it's on e-mail too. "Take the pie out of the freezer and put it in the oven." *She bought ten, on special. Pie three nights in a row. That's seven pies to go. No vegetables. I wouldn't eat them, but they should be there.*

He cooked up two-minute noodles, hacked off a slab of cheese and emptied the tin of Milo into a liter of milk.

Ned had a pile of homework—math, English, science—but at seven o'clock he was still watching TV; half-listening, waiting, annoyed now. At himself. At her. At everything.

Pow! Pow! Pow! The bullets ripped through the running man and he dropped like a sack.

"Turn that TV *off*!"

Ah ha! She's home. I stir from my slumber on the rock.

"What?"

"You heard!"

He was in the mood for a fight. He chucked the big cushions near the TV and turned the sound down.

She was clattering in the kitchen. "Oh, you didn't put the *pie* in the oven!"

"What?"

"The *pie*! Are you *deaf*? Have you done your home-work?"

"Yeah."

"When?"

"Before."

"Well, why is your bag here, zipped up where you dropped it with your stinking shoes and everything in this *mess* by the back door?"

"I said I've *done* it."

Warming up fast!

2

"I hope you haven't downloaded any games."

More sink and stove noises.

"You're in year seven now, you know. *Oh!*" she exclaimed, annoyed, and appeared in the doorway, waving a yogurt carton. "Did you toss this? There's still a whole lot left in here."

"So?"

"Do you think we're *rich*? And this container can be *recycled*! God, and we're trying to save the world for the next generation! The next generation doesn't give a fig! And *turn* that TV *off*!"

"Oh, come on, Mum. This is Real Life TV. Stuff that really happened."

"*OFF!*"

The car fell again in slow motion. A body hit the ground, moved slightly and lay still.

"I *don't want* those pictures in my home."

"What's wrong with them?"

"They've made entertainment out of pain and death."

"Everybody watches it. Get real."

I am rising like a cobra about to strike.

"*OFF!*"

"You're forty-two, Mum. You're ancient. You don't know a thing."

Suddenly, like a berserk ten-pin bowler, she swung in from the kitchen with the cast-iron frying pan and flung it at the screen with all her might.

Ned hurled himself to the side with a cushion over his head. The handle of the frying pan hit the cop's fat cheek.

A deep *thudBANG!* The TV screen imploded into the vacuum, then exploded. Splinters of glass sprayed

3

everywhere. A couple of sparks, then a slight powder residue settled.

"What are you *doing*?" he shrieked.

"I turned it *OFF*!" she screamed back. She was shaking like jelly. "That's live TV for you. That's *REAL LIFE TV*!"

"My *GOD*, what's got *YOU*?" He picked splinters of glass from his windbreaker. "You're lucky I can still *see*!"

Her face was white and lined. Her glasses went downhill on her nose. He was suddenly scared.

She's gone loony!

"*That* got your face out of the screen." She was breathing fast, and her voice wavered. "You tell *me* to get a life! *You* get a life! That's your life, a screen. If it's not the TV, it's the blinking computer."

"So? You got me the first games, remember? And what do you care, anyway? You wouldn't know if I'm here or not. You didn't even come home till half past eight last night, in case you didn't notice!" He picked up the frying pan. "Now who's violent?" he slung at her.

She covered her face with her hands. "It's so *brutal*. Killing in cold blood. And you think it's entertaining. You're thirteen. *You* don't know a darn thing."

"Yes, it's me, isn't it?" shouted Ned, his chin stuck forward as if inviting a punch. "Everything I watch is *junk*. Everything I listen to is *crap*. Everything I do is *wrong*." He hunched his shoulders, arms crossed. He was shaking.

The TV looked bizarre. Where the screen had been was a shadow mask, a metallic sheet creased like dented foil. Ned gingerly unplugged the set.

Her voice changed. "I'm sorry, Ned. I'm sorry, Ned. I'm so sorry."

She spent an age picking up the glass, and vacuumed till the noise nearly drove him crazy. Then there was silence.

"Don't tell anyone," she said quietly.

"What?"

"What happened to the TV."

"You expect me to say it suicided?" *Good one.*

She stood there clutching her pale face.

Ned brushed past, snatched up the remote from the table as if it was a symbol of victory and slammed out the back door. But it was an empty victory. He had a pain in the guts.

He climbed into the netting cage in the corner of the yard. His lizards were piled on top of each other in their favorite spot—a tunnel of rotting ironbark. He picked out the oldest blue-tongue, Fred, and held him to the warmth of his chest. Then for a long time he just sat quietly, in a sort of blank despair.

"She's going nuts, Fred. She's going nuts."

Ned and Janet circled around each other in the quiet house.

She's drifting like a ghost, except she doesn't go through walls.

"You're seriously weird."

She stood still. "Don't say that. It's not funny."

"You're scared it's true, aren't you?" He studied her.

She reached out to touch him.

"Leave me alone. You're like a rash!"

Then she flipped. "Put the rubbish out, you lazy little sod, and do the dishes for a change. You never do anything. The place is a dump."

"So?"

"You'll have to get on with real people one day, you know, not just flickering phantoms on a screen."

"*You* have to get on with real people too! Like *me*, for example."

He took a muesli bar into her study and shut the door. This was where she did all her work on trees and forests. Usually it was tidy, but an unsteady mound of magazines and papers balanced on a pile of books. Ned settled himself in front of her powerful computer.

At least she won't smash this one.

A big, clear picture snapped up—the opening image of *Quuad*.

The barrel of his weapon bobbed at the bottom of the screen as he twisted through the station, quickly blasting his way to a higher level. He was stirred up and scored well.

No way will I do homework tonight!

Then Janet opened the door and stood watching him.

He held up one of the nearest books. "*Test Your Own Mental Health*. Is this for real?"

"It's for work."

"Testing the mental health of *trees*?"

"Well, if you know the facts…" She faltered.

"You want to know if you're going nuts. Why don't you just say it?" He blasted his way down the steel corridor.

If you want my opinion, you are.

She didn't say anything for a full minute. Dancing around the screen, he took out four in rapid fire.

"Ned?"

"What?"

"I want you to call your father."

Ned couldn't sleep that night. In the darkness, he heard Monty and Python, his Cunningham skinks, scrambling around the aquarium beside his bed.

I'm not going to live with him, Monty. Mum and I are the family. When we went to the zoo, she said, "No use buying a family ticket. One adult, one child is cheaper. In terms of a family, Ned, we're it." That's what she said. "We're it."

Usually, even after a fight, they kissed goodnight when he went to bed. It was understood that they had each other. But now he wasn't sure. About anything.

She's just stressed. That's all.

Bad Day

Janet was usually at work in the study long before Ned got up, but next morning her bedroom door was shut. Ned ate his Weet-Bix alone, experimenting with the cloud of tiny bugs that hovered over the fruit bowl. The TV looked like some weird modern sculpture.

Before he left for school, he knocked on Janet's door. "Bye, Mum."

No reply. Just a grunt.

She's giving me the silent treatment.

He slammed the back door and set off.

Skip school? Haven't done my homework. Thurley'll give me heaps. French? Non merci, Mrs. Hudson. Je suis invisible. Simmo in math hasn't got time to scratch himself; he won't even remember the homework...yeah, I'll go see Sean.

Sean had been Ned's best friend ever since kindergarten. Same Batman capes, same bikes, same skateboards, same jokes that no one else got. But in junior high, Sean had made friends with Huxley—one of the sharp, cool guys. They always sat on the steps at the back of the gym. Ned hung around, but he was quiet and they thought he was a bit weird.

They were talking about e-mail names. "Ubolt101." "Vulcha." "Yeah, that's cool." "Chill666." "Dechamp."

"So, what's yours, Ned?"

"Herpman."

They cracked up. "Aargh, he's diseased! Don't touch him!"

"No, it's the study of snakes—herpetology. It means 'Snakeman.'"

But they didn't listen. He looked at Sean, but he was laughing too. He used to think the name was cool.

"Ever seen a TV explode?" He threw it in—hurt but still trying.

"You're not allowed to dump TVs that aren't smashed because they're dangerous. There's a vacuum in the tube."

"Well, I've seen one explode."

"Bull!"

"Our TV at home."

"You're lying!"

He had their attention.

"My aunt smashed it with a frying pan. It was so cool."

"You couldn't break it with a frying pan. You'd have to use a hammer and hit it bloody hard."

"She did, with a frying pan."

"Oh yeah. Sure she did. Aunts do that all the time."

"Take that, you naughty TV!"

They laughed at him again.

"I've got the remote." He took it out of his pocket. It looked ridiculous in the schoolyard. They laughed harder. He pointed the remote at them like a weapon and pressed Stop.

"Your aunt's as cracked in the head as you are!"

Ned turned and walked away.

"Hey, Herpman, change channels!"

"Watch out for your auntie! She'll get you with the frying pan!"

"If this remote worked, you'd be dead!"

A flood of shame and betrayal washed through him.

It's not my bloody aunt, it's Mum. Why did I tell those morons? I don't want anyone to know, especially not them.

Last class of the day. Information Technology. They were meant to work in pairs, but no one chose Ned, so he was put with the new girl. "You're not supposed to do that. That's not what Mr. Watson said. You'll break it…." Someone came back from music and she moved.

Ned. Dead. Deadhead. Delete. These computers are crap.

Mr. Watson was telling them how to create some graph.

Bet I know more than he does anyway.

Ned sat in front of the computer, immobile except for his fingers, and tapped in Herpman. He made the word bold and black, then he stretched it until it filled the screen. Then he selected the dynamite and blew it up. He typed another name, small, in chunky black letters, and centered it:

Remote Man

He dawdled home. Checked out the computer shop to see if they had the new game yet. No point in hurrying to catch his favorite TV shows. From three houses away he could see the rear of their truck sticking out of the garage.

She's home already!

The house was strangely dark.

"Mum?"

Gingerly, he knocked on her bedroom door and pushed

it open. The blind was drawn, and in the gloom he could make out her shape curled up on the bed with the comforter over her head.

"Mum?"

He pulled back the comforter and cringed from what he saw.

Argh! Sea monster dredged up in the nets!

Eyes swollen, wet hair plastered against her cheek, her body shaking with silent sobs.

"Mum, what's *wrong*?"

She rolled over to face the wall, pulled a pillow over her head and began to cry aloud.

"What's *wrong*? What is it?"

He touched her arm. She flinched away.

"Please stop crying."

She hadn't gone to work, she hadn't eaten, the toilet paper was a ribbon on the bathroom floor, the phone dangled from the kitchen bench like something at the scene of a crime.

Oh God! Oh God please! What do I do? It's not an act. She's been crying all day. Oh God. What do I do? Helena. Call Helena in the Northern Territory. She'll know.

He found the address book and searched for his aunt's name. The numbers swam on the page.

They talk for hours on Sunday nights. Northern Territory…Helena? Yes…Home?…No, work…Wakwak Community School…

He dialed. So many numbers. Three times he got it wrong. Then it was ringing.

Please answer…please…

"Helena speaking."

"Oh, thank God!"

"What is it, Ned? I left my class, so I can't talk long."

"Helena, I think Mum's…"

"What, Ned?"

"I think she's…lost it."

"What do you mean?"

"She's crying and crying and crying. She won't stop." He traced the pen round a slight groove in the wooden bench.

"Is she hurt? Injured?"

"No, nothing like that."

"Can she talk?"

"I think so, but…she won't say anything to me."

"Ned, can you think of a reason why she's like this?"

He swallowed and said it. "Me. I got detentions and mucked around, and we've had fights. Last night she smashed the TV."

He heard her take a deep breath. "What happened?"

He told her.

She paused. Ned could hear crows in the background and kids yelling.

"Can I speak to her?"

"You can try."

Ned listened on the kitchen phone. Helena asked questions steadily. His mother replied weakly through the sobs: "I don't know why…I'm so miserable…wish I could disappear…."

"Helena. It's me, Ned."

"Oh, Ned. She's not good. I'll call the minute I get home this afternoon. You have to get a doctor. Dr. Liddell. In the phone book. Then make your mum a cup of tea. Look after her."

"What's wrong with her?"

"I don't know. She's very unhappy."

He knotted his fingers in the phone cord. "How do you fix that?"

"Well, there are pills, other things they can do. She needs a break…."

"From?"

"Work."

"Me?"

"Maybe you too. But it's not your fault. I'm sorry, Ned, but I really must go. Try not to worry. I'll phone tonight. And remember, it's not your fault. Do you hear that?"

"Yes."

"What did I say?"

"It's not my fault."

"Right. Think you can cope?"

"Yeah," said Ned, uncertain.

"Good man." Click.

Of course it's my fault.

He could hear his mother's voice ringing in his ears: "You drive me *nuts!*"

Talk, talk, talk

Dr. Liddell didn't look like a doctor. She was younger than his mother, with a cheerful face. She was calm and firm. She organized Janet into the shower and a clean bed. She organized small bottles of expensive pills to be taken morning and evening.

And Helena organized Agnes, a distant cousin, to look after them. Janet and Ned rarely had visitors, and now there was a stranger cooking chicken on their grill.

"I'm getting stuck into this place," she told a friend on the phone. "It's full of dead flowers and rotting fruit, and *lizards!*"

The one room Agnes didn't tackle was the study. She looked at all Janet's treasures but didn't touch a thing. She studied the photo of Janet and Ned. Janet stood straight in her comfortable shoes, shirt collar out over her sensible sweater. Beside her slouched Ned, his baggy trousers crunkled over disintegrating Nikes, battered skateboard under his arm.

"Opposites," thought Agnes. She closed the door and tackled the oven.

Agnes dumped the old faithful TV into a Dumpster in the alley, covered the low table where it had been with a cloth and set a vase of artificial flowers in the center.

Shrine in memory. RIP TV.

There was a message on the answering machine.

"Janet—it's Max. Where are you?"

Ned phoned his mum's boss.

"What's going on?" said Max.

"She's…not very well."

"She didn't look very flash. What's wrong?"

"She's depressed."

"Oh boy!" he groaned. "Did she tell you what happened last month? Her computer crashed and she lost a heap of data and the results from a test. She was working late and hadn't backed up. Wouldn't be so bad, except we're coming up for a funding review and the government might pull the plug on us. She's been trying to catch up…."

"Her computer *crashed*?"

"Yes," sighed Max. "Wonderful things, computers."

Ned lay on his back in bed with the remote in the center of his chest.

The computer crashed. She crashed.

When he lost some of his lizard project last year, he felt like kicking in the computer. Then he remembered the little sad face in the center of the Mac screen when the school library computer died.

He pressed buttons on the remote.

Rewind. Tears leap back into eyes. TV zaps back whole. Frying pan un-flings. Pause.

He held his breath…but his body gasped for air.

Dr. Liddell talked to Ned. They sat at the table in the strangely clean kitchen. Dr. Liddell was smiley. Ned was suspicious.

"How's school, Ned?"

15

"Okay."

"Do your friends know about your mother?"

"No way." He stared at his hands in silence.

Man, if they found out, there'd be a feeding frenzy: "Oh cool! Ned's mum's gone mad! Sensational! What did she do? Burn the house down?"

"Will she get better?"

"I'm sure she will, Ned. You know, many people find it hard to go on at some stage in life, but nobody talks about it. It's like a hidden illness."

Ned listened, not seeing anything.

"Your father wants you to go and stay with him. Helena and Agnes think it's a good idea."

"No way."

"It will help your mother if she knows you're safe and happy and well."

"Pretty hard being happy," said Ned.

"I know," she sighed.

"I'm staying here."

"Well, you could be right, Ned. Your mother says she wants you to go, but I think, deep down, she wants you to stay."

Dr. Liddell studied his pale, gawky face. He was so self-contained. She knew he'd taken on the shopping and some cooking and was going to school.

"Ned, I'll be straight with you, and I wouldn't say this to most kids. It's like...what's it like?" She gazed out the window, searching for inspiration. "Ever seen kelp growing?"

"Seaweed?"

"Yes. Kelp grows in long brown straps, like ribbons,

16

which stream out and are swept by the waves and the surge of the sea. Now, at the bottom of the kelp there's like…a strong arm, which ends in a foot, which is stuck to the rocks. Well, Ned, I think for her, right now, you're that foot attached to the rocks. I guess what I'm saying is, 'Hang on. You're doing a good job.'"

Ned spent long hours at the computer in Janet's study, opposite a photograph of Huon pines in a forest somewhere in Tasmania—some place called Harrison's Knot. She found it while identifying vegetation from aerial photographs; then she hiked there. It took three days. She used to say, "When you're older and strong enough, Ned, we'll walk in to Harrison's Knot."

We'll never go there now. I'm the foot of a piece of kelp!

He turned on the modem and looked up "kelp" on Yahoo! There were 28,583 related sites. He clicked on a couple and bookmarked the Macroalgae Harvesters site, which had an interesting format.

Ned was amazed by the amount of e-mail his mother received from scientist friends all around the world. They swapped articles, information and thoughts about all kinds of things.

Must be a great long-distance friend. Just not too hot at real life.

Ned appointed himself Janet's e-mail officer. He printed out the messages, stapled the pages together, clipped each day's into a bundle, put them in a folder and showed them to Janet, but she didn't want to know.

By the end of the first week, the e-mail dropped off as people waited for a reply, but Chris in Tucson, Arizona, USA, kept asking direct questions.

"Why the silence? Have you had the big breakthrough? Press conferences? Hungover from too much champagne?"

Missed the target there, Christine old girl.

Then: "You okay? What's happening? I'm sure there's a good reason, Jan, but I really want to know what's going on? Is Ned okay?"

He liked Chris. He began to tap out a reply, one foot on the desk, balancing his breakfast.

Dear Chris,
Mum's sick.

Now what do I say?

Sometimes the phone rang in the middle of the night and Ned blundered into the study to answer it. It would be another colleague, wondering about Janet.

"She's having a few health problems."

They always wanted to know more.

That night, Ned found himself in the study, wide awake at two o'clock in the morning. He clicked on the computer. The start-up chord was friendly, comforting. He drummed his fingers to the singsong spacey sounds as the Internet connection was made. Password, Mailbox, then—out of the blue, an e-mail for him!

Ned, Kuz

Sorry about your mum. Hope she gets UNmegga bulk stressed
V V V V V V V V V V V V V V V V V Vsoon.

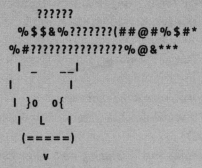

```
            ??????
        % $ $ & %???????(# # @ # % $ #*
      % #?????????????????% @ & * * *
        |  _     __|
        |          |
        |  }o   o{
        |   L    |
         (= = = = =)
              v
```

Mymumyouraunt says she will get better.
I met you twice.
Uno wedding Sydney we sA t down the front craking thin crayfish
legs & sucking thm out until some BOSSY relo draggedus off
because we were making TOO MCUH NOISE!!!!! peeple coulnn't
hear the BOOORRING spitches? That was me dragged off with you
Duo Christmas Melbourne. This was MOLTO BUG DEAL because
we flew down for the holidays. All us kids were shy then *JUST*
when we got good friends HO HO HO VERY FUNNY LETS GO
MAD& weclimb that HUMBNUNNNGEOUS pine tree in the park
nextxdoor we had to go rEMEMBER?
You like sssssssssssssssssssssssssssnakes don't you?

Kuza
CROCLAND

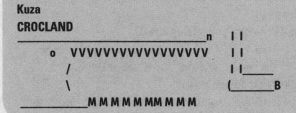

```
_____n    | |
    o   VVVVVVVVVVVVVVVVVV       | |
      /                          | |_____
      \                          (_____B
_____M M M M M MM M M M
```

Helena's daughter. What a weirdo! I remember that Christmas.

He read it through four times, grinning; then he clicked around the Net, feeling unexplainably lighter. He discovered a new game site and played checkers until the boy in Alaska left abruptly.

Remote Man has entered the chat room.

Ned had watched chat plenty of times, but he'd never actually talked.

Like jumping into a skipping rope. Wise guys joking, flirting. Random. Catchy, sexy, corny. Scraps.

The chat rolled up like little waves in shallow water. Then a strange voice entered, talking straight to *him!*

theSythe: Oh Remote Man Great NAME!! Why do you call yourself Remote Man?
Remote Man: I haven't the remotest idea.
theSythe: Remote events triggered from afar?
Remote Man: Yes
theSythe: You are my BROTHER!
Remote Man: How?
theSythe: REMOTE MAN! you are my BROTHER REMOTE MAN you and me press the buttons pull the triggers from the distant mountain
Remote Man: What are you talking about?
theSythe: I have rung the bells I have set the charges I have struck the match and the fuses are BURNING
Remote Man: What do you mean?
theSythe: To take out the MOCKERS Remote Man THEY DON'T WANT US we will have REVENGE their blood will stream in the

20

The chat room curdled. Many chatters left. Others tapped in things like: "Tut, tut, tut!" "Back in the coffin, Dracula" "Whooa boy!!!!!!!!!!!!!!" "Nurse, come and get him!"

Somewhere a tortured brain sat alone, like Ned, face lit by the computer screen, pouring out venom. Ned clicked off. He was sweating, shaken and frightened.

Oh man, I wanted remote power too but that's scary! That's a freaky brain out of control. I'm like a little kid afraid of monsters in the dark.

Then he clicked back and re-read Kate's e-mail, to help return to normal. He tapped a reply, but it wasn't the crazy one he'd planned to send earlier.

Kuza,
Yes I like reptiles. I have two Cunningham skinks called Monty
and Python, twelve blue-tongue lizards and two stumpy-tails.
They're hibernating. That Christmas—were you the kid who
wouldn't come down from the top of the tree? There's a python
called the Oenpelli python where you live. Have you seen one?
Remote Man

He read Kate's e-mail seven times before he finally

logged off that night. But in the dark, the voice of theSythe snarled in his head and he couldn't sleep.

The nights were hard, but the days were livable. Ned was managing. He found out that the proper word for the kelp foot was the "holdfast."

Hold fast, Holdfast.

He became quite talkative with his mother, sitting in the chair by her bed. They had a game with the remote, where he'd point it at her and click and she'd do things. But he had to be careful with this remote game, or a wrinkle would appear in her chin and she'd cry.

How many tears could a person cry? The bin by her bed overflowed with tissues full of tears, and she hated tissues. "Waste of good trees," she said. Ned remembered how she used to drive miles to demonstrations and rallies, trying to save native forests, and sent off letters to politicians like a whirlwind. She used to be such a fighter. She used to be so strong she could walk to Harrison's Knot.

Helena called from Wakwak most evenings. She'd have a quick chat with Ned and a long talk with Janet.

Then one evening, after the phone call, Janet suddenly announced in a matter-of-fact voice that he was going away.

"Here, Ned," she said, reaching out for his arm. "You're flying up north for a few weeks to stay with Helena, Ray and Kate."

He tried to smile. "But you need me here."

"I'm going to stay with Agnes."

But I'm the holdfast! I don't want anybody to go anywhere. I don't want you to go to boring Agnes's. I don't want to go to the Northern Territory. Why do you want me out of the way?

"…Ray's a rough diamond. He's got a temper and swears like a trooper, but he'd give you the shirt off his back."

So it was all worked out. Ned took Monty and Python to a kid down the street. He didn't know if he could trust him, but he had no choice.

Agnes's husband took Ned to the airport and left him with an airline attendant who checked his name on a list and told him to sit and wait.

Unaccompanied minor.

Behind him, a man talked brightly to his girlfriend on a mobile phone. Ned watched a mother and father with their little son between them, walking along holding hands. "One. Two. Threeeee!" and they swung the kid up. With a sudden rush of sadness, Ned remembered doing that, and he missed his mother the way she used to be.

He stared at his reflection in the huge glass window. Everyone else was moving and happy. He was still, surrounded by strangers. Remote Man. He couldn't see his eyes; they were dark hollows in his reflected face.

"May I have your attention please, flight number 315 to Darwin has been delayed. Please wait for a further announcement."

His eyes burned.

I am thirteen. I have not cried for a long time. I will not cry now.

He set his face in a snakelike mask and tipped his head back, but the tears spilled down. He couldn't help it. Everything he cared about seemed to be peeling away.

4

The Top End

"Hi, Kuz."

The minute Ned saw Kate, he remembered her, but she was still a shock. She was six months older than him and looked as wild as her e-mails. Her straight blond hair stuck out in defiant tufts; her face was alive, brown and grinning hard. A ready-made cousin-friend.

Helena gave him a solid hug, which normally he would have hated, but he stood and took it. She was hot but had a nice mint-tree smell.

"Good to have you up here, mate." Ray's big paw squashed his hand. Ray had blue paint in his fingernails.

The sticky heat was a shock. Kate was a shock. Everything was a shock.

"Do you know what NT stands for?" said Kate. "Not today. Not tomorrow."

"She's warm all right," said Ray. "Going to hit ninety-five degrees."

Ned stumbled along with them in a daze, giddy from the plane and the heat.

Ray drove fast. There was no speed limit in the Northern Territory and he made good time on the sealed highway. Then, about ten miles from Wakwak, the highway became a two-lane gravel road, and then the road became a single rough track. The corrugations shook every nut and bolt in the car. Talk was impossible.

The small town of Wakwak was another shock.

Rubbish blew everywhere, and tongues of fire had left blackened patches of burnt grass. In the distance, the ragged blue cliff of the escarpment was the backdrop to a huge billabong, where the sun glistened on the broad stretch of water. Ned saw a water monitor dart from a rock.

Kate's dog, Minga, barked a welcome. Their house was built on stilts. From outside it looked boring, perched like an insect in a dry scrappy garden, but inside it was like a den—dark and fascinating, rich with their personalities.

"Take your shoes off," said Kate, tossing her sandals on the pile by the door. The polished wood felt cool and smooth underfoot. Ned soon found that despite all the comforts—the air conditioning, the impressive art books and souvenirs from around the world—he was still in danger of standing on a frog or being bitten suddenly by an ant.

Everything was screen-printed with Aboriginal designs—the curtains, the tablecloth, the bedspreads and the cushions on the cane chairs—and fine hand-woven baskets were used to store all sorts of things.

Ned shared the spare room with the computer, Helena's sewing stuff, Ray's paintings, and enough food for four months in an enormous freezer. There was a fan on the ceiling.

Ray took him aside. "Do us a favor, Ned. Don't go playing dare games with Kate. We had friends up here at Christmas, and she broke her wrist swinging off the water tower, and the time before that we had to wait three-quarters of an hour while she swam back across the gorge at Jim Jim Falls."

"Help yourself to a cool drink anytime," said Helena.

The fridge stored Helena's makeup, ointment, medicine, film, chocolate, Vegemite, shaving cream, all sorts of odd things.

Ned went to the toilet and when he stood up, the seat rose with him. It dropped down with an embarrassing *WHACK!*

"Toilet seat stick to your sweaty bum?" laughed Kate.

Ned blushed. It was all so rough and rude and *hot*.

That afternoon, Ned asked to check his e-mail. He showed Kate how to get around the Web, introduced her to the Net, to chat rooms, his favorite games in Tin Pan Alley, his favorite sites.

"This is so *cool!*" said Kate.

She's a natural.

In the evening, they joined a strange promenade when the balanders, as the white Australians were called, came out into the slightly cooler air and walked their dogs around the billabong. The fearsome camp dogs ignored Kate and Minga, but they knew Ned was an easy target.

"Pick up a stick and chuck it at 'em," yelled Kate, unfazed. "If they give you heaps, give 'em heaps back."

Ned saw a goanna and plenty of other lizard tracks in the sand. Kate knew lots of general stuff, but Ned was the expert on reptiles.

"You're the only balander I know who's really happy when he sees a snake," said Kate.

"Ever seen an Oenpelli python?"

Kate pulled the silliest wide-eyed face at him.

Ned had never met any Aboriginal kids before Kate proudly introduced him.

"This is my best cousin, Ned."

"Your *only* cousin," said Ned.

The kids stared at him, shuffling their bare feet in the

sand, and shoved each other and laughed, but it was okay. Ned tried to say some of their words, and they shrieked with laughter.

Sounds like talking with marbles in your mouth.

"Kunwinjku at home. At school we learn English," said one of the boys.

"The Wakwak kids look...I dunno...cool," said Ned after dinner that night.

"Yeah, makes you feel uncooked, doesn't it?" said Kate.

Ned put his white arm beside her brown arm.

"Well, if *you* feel uncooked, imagine how *I* feel."

"Give you an arm wrestle!"

"Me and Mum used to arm wrestle," said Ned.

Kate's hand was hot and sweaty. She won, but it was close.

Whenever the phone rang, Ned listened for news from home. Once he overheard Ray talking about him: "...a remote little city ratbag. Needs a good kick up the backside. Won't talk much, but I watch him a bit an' I'm thinkin': 'Now hold on, there's a lot going on here.' You should see him on the computer. He's like bloody Tarzan swinging through the jungle. He's giving Kate a guided tour of the universe inside that thing. His mother's had a rough trot. Hope she'll make it good again."

"Put your boots on. We're off."

It was very early Saturday morning and Kate was full of energy.

"Where? It's only six-thirty!"

"Mind your business." She poked out her tongue. "Fill your drink bottle. Come on!" she insisted. "Before it gets hot."

It was a tricky job getting the bikes through the gate in the high cyclone fence without Minga slipping through too. Ned glanced back. Minga's eyes said "traitors."

They rode down the avenue of huge dark-leafed mango trees that ran through the town. In the deep shade, silhouetted against the plains, a kid leapt around trying to catch something beside the road. He stood straight and watched them ride up. The knees in his skinny legs reminded Ned of knots in a stick.

"Philemon, this is Ned."

The boy nodded but didn't look up. He said something in marble-talk.

"What did he say?"

"Hot potatoes," grinned Kate.

"Where are we going?"

"There and back." She was mighty pleased about something.

Kate and Philemon took turns riding each other on the old bike. They rode like a couple of clowns, easy and funny, Kate hanging on to Philemon's shoulders and Philemon's stick-legs pedaling like crazy. Then Kate grunted as she pedaled, with Philemon saying things, laughing and doing hand signals. Kate was strong. Ned was having enough trouble pushing himself along, let alone riding somebody else.

The day pack with the water bottle bumped uncomfortably, and Ned's back was a pool of sweat. He got off and walked through the sand drifts. The other two always rode until the very last second of balance, just saving themselves, screaming and laughing, before they toppled sideways.

They rode for ages toward the escarpment. Then they left the bikes and the gravel road and set off on foot, trudging through prickly scrub. Something bounded away from them. Philemon raced after it, the pink soles of his feet flashing.

"Much farther?"

"Half as much and twice again."

Why did I ask?

They picked their way through the stones and the dry crackling bush, toward the rocky outcrop at the base of the escarpment. Philemon fluttered his fingers at them, signaling, "Be quiet! Very quiet!"

They crept forward. Philemon froze. Slowly and deliberately, he pointed. Ned couldn't see a thing. Kate shoved him forward and pointed. Still nothing. With her hands she lined up his head. Then his eyes clicked on it.

Snakes alive! An Oenpelli python!

Motionless near a horizontal crack in the rocks lay a magnificent pale brown python. It was delicately patterned and easily twelve feet long. Ned stood with his mouth open, a half-smile of wonder on his face.

"We found it for you," whispered Kate, glowing with pleasure. "Philemon's mob told us it was up here. Mum and Dad would freak out if they knew. This is close to sacred ground, but Philemon's uncle reckons it's okay. We've seen it three times. That's its favorite rock. They're hard to find."

"I know. They're nocturnal and white people didn't know about them until 1977."

"Well, they never asked."

"This is really rare. People hardly ever see them; they're docile, and the scalation…"

"Don't give me all that professor stuff," said Kate.

Philemon said something in Kunwinjku.

"Eats rock-wallabies," translated Kate.

They watched the python for five minutes; then Ned inched closer. Sensing danger, the python lifted its head and slid smoothly into a crack in the rocks.

5

The Cowboy

Dolobbo, the Aboriginal art center, was a low building with a long shady veranda on one side where the artists sat cross-legged and painted their bark paintings. Inside, in a big work room with a huge table, Ray supervised the screen-printing. The Aboriginal elders employed him because they knew he was an excellent craftsman as well as a talented painter.

Ned watched, fascinated, as the paint, like runny butter, was squeegeed through the screen. Then came the moment of truth when the screen was lifted to reveal bold purple anteaters on green, or a river of black lizards on red, or bush tucker in black on yellow.

The screen had to be positioned accurately, so the pattern flowed, and the thick colored inks had to be just the right consistency, so they printed evenly. There were many tricks to the trade.

Most of the printed fabric went in rolls to Darwin or the tourist shop in Kakadu, but Dolobbo sold some to the visitors who made the journey to Wakwak.

In the hottest part of the day, when the sun burned relentlessly in the blue-gray sky and the camp dogs shambled instead of trotted, there were two good places to keep cool. The first was Ned's room, with the fan and the air conditioner in the lounge on high; the other was the Dolobbo shop.

"Always a beautiful eighty-two degrees," said Geraldine, who worked there. She didn't take slackers. "You're not just hangin' around here and yackin'. Tidy up."

Even with two doors to the outside, it still got dusty, and customers left a mess—not that there were many visitors. To reach Wakwak, you had to cross the East Alligator river into Arnhem Land, so you had to know the tides, and you needed a permit.

"Each artist has their own story, which belongs to them," Kate explained to Ned as she refolded fabric, "and that's what they paint. Tourists love those stories. 'Member that old American bloke, Geraldine, who wrote the whole story down? '*Wonn*erful! *Wonn*erful! *Wonn*erful!' 'Member him? He said '*wonn*erful' about fifty times."

Ned hid his two favorite X-ray snake paintings at the back of a pile so they wouldn't sell.

Ray blustered in, wearing a tattered T-shirt and looking hot and bothered. "You here?" He was particularly grumpy. "You can stay if you like, but I get one interruption and you're *out*, okay? We've been trying to get onto this new screen for a week."

The workroom door slammed behind him.

Then the visitors arrived. Ned, who was angling for an invitation to go catching file snakes in the billabong, stopped mid-sentence.

The American swaggered into Dolobbo and sized it up as if he was going to buy it. His clothes hung with a fashionable looseness. There were pockets all over them, and his linen trousers set him apart—the only person for a hundred miles who wasn't wearing shorts. There was something larger-than-life about him. A younger man with short hair followed him in.

Impressive. The Cowboy has just entered the saloon. And he wants something.

"We want to see large paintings," said the Cowboy. "*Important* paintings."

They had arrived unannounced, making things difficult. Serious buyers usually called before they flew in, to give Geraldine time to select a range of paintings for them to look at, and Ray the chance to put on a clean shirt.

Geraldine began to show him the larger pictures, but she was uneasy, as if she couldn't stand the glare of his attention. Ned thought maybe the stranger couldn't understand her, so when she dropped into an awkward silence, he took over. Kate was strangely quiet, her lips thin.

Ned surprised himself. He showed the stranger the paintings and told a couple of stories that Geraldine had told him. He felt important. The other man wasn't interested. He sat thumbing through magazines, glancing at his watch from time to time.

Ned's favorite X-ray snake painting came to light. The Cowboy studied it closely. "Gee, now isn't that beautiful?"

"Yeah."

"Now what actual type of snake would that be?"

"A serpent in an Aboriginal story."

"My, this is the most wonderful country for snakes."

"Yeah," enthused Ned. "It's got a python named after it, the Oenpelli python."

"Is that right?" said the man.

"I've seen it."

"No *kiddin'*!" The American suddenly turned on the charm and listened attentively. "That'd be down by the waterhole."

"No, near the escarpment about four miles from here."

"The escarpment?"

"At the foot of the closest knob, there's a rock platform."

"Well, lucky you. Not much interested in snakes

33

myself." The smile was turned off. "What do you think?" He showed the younger man the painting.

"Too small."

The stranger held up a bark painting of a kangaroo.

Ned began, "When the old man kangaroo—" but the Cowboy rudely cut him short.

"Don't give me that spiel. You got a book or somethin'?"

The remark hit Ned like a slap in the face. He blushed with humiliation and shut up.

"Put these seven paintings against that wall."

Geraldine did as she was told; then the Cowboy stood back and cracked his knuckles. "Now, the matter of price."

"The prices are marked on them," said Kate.

"I need to talk with someone about that."

"Should I get Ray?" Ned whispered to Geraldine, his eyes flicking to the workshop door.

"Go get Ray," boomed the Cowboy.

"He doesn't want to be interrupted," said Kate firmly, weighing up his anger against her father's.

The Cowboy glared at her, and pushed his way through the workshop door. "Anyone here know somethin' useful about these pictures?"

"He bought seven major paintings and paid cash. That'll keep everyone in smokes for a while. This has been a very good day for Dolobbo and I, for one, am going to celebrate." Ray poured himself a long cold lime drink. "You did a good job, kids."

"I wish we hadn't sold him a thing!" said Kate.

"Oh, come on." Ray was exasperated. "What am I supposed to do? Ask customers to fill in a bloody niceness questionnaire? Get real. It's hard enough to make ends meet as it is. Dolobbo's a business, remember."

"Must have a mansion," said Ned.

"He'll *sell* them," said Kate. "He wasn't even *interested* in them, not one tiny paint dot, which is strange because usually dealers *are* very interested. And did you see the way he drove off? Chucked a screaming U-ie and burned up past the clinic like Bruce Willis. Nearly hit one of the dogs."

"Who were they?" asked Helena.

Ray stretched his arms. "Couple of septics. The buyer was a snappy dresser. Never caught his name. Paid cash. Got their own plane and a flash four-wheel drive. Permit to travel in Arnhem Land studying rocks."

"Geologists?"

"Geologists, my arse," said Kate. "Rip-offologists."

"You watch your bloody language, girl," said Ray.

Ned kept quiet.

Kate got a handle on him. I felt such a fool. He squashed me like a cockroach. Creep.

A grudge settled down inside him. A wariness.

Mango Tree

Ned spent three weeks in Wakwak. Early each morning, he and Kate were driven across the East Alligator river to wait beside the dusty road for the school bus to Kakadu. Every night, he spoke to his mother on the phone. It was good to hear her voice, and he always tried to make her laugh.

Helena nailed him now and then for a little chat. She wanted to know about her sister's life. They talked about how persistent she was, and how a scientist's career was difficult, and about her passion for trees.

"...but now she just sits around. Even getting out of bed is hard for her."

"We'll get her back on deck," said Helena, making it sound like a cheerful conspiracy.

But Kate was the one Ned really talked to. She was tough and harebrained, but he trusted her. Perched up in the dark trees among the mangoes, which hung like huge green yoyos, he told her things he had never told anyone else.

"Does your mum have boyfriends?" asked Kate.

"You're joking!" said Ned.

"What happened to your dad?"

"Well, Mum's doing research—*was* doing research—on die-back in gum trees...."

"Die-back?"

"It's something that makes trees turn brown and die. She's desperate to find out why it happens, because forests are dying."

"Yes, but your dad?"

"Well, everything at home got die-back because of

36

die-back. The house got die-back, things in the fridge got die-back, her cooking got die-back, their relationship got die-back."

"Your dad turned brown?"

Ned snorted. "No, he was organized right out of the die-back by this pepped-up travel agent doll. They live in New Zealand now."

"Kiwi witch," said Kate.

"No, she's an Aussie."

Ned reached out and pulled off a green mango. "I'm never going to get married."

"I probably will," said Kate. "Someone to arm wrestle, who doesn't care if I fart. Someone to keep me warm if I ever ever ever in my life get cold."

"What if you don't get cold?"

"Someone to wave the fan."

"You wish!" He laughed and threw the mango at her. Quick as a flash, she caught it.

"Why do you call yourself Remote Man?"

"I have powers to do things from afar," he said in a horror-movie voice, but there was a hint of something deeper and she didn't laugh.

"What powers?"

"You'll see."

And she accepted that too. "Well, you're good at the computer."

They sat in silence for a while.

"I was Remote *Girl* when I was a baby." Then she took on a serious newsreader's voice: "'Kate Spokes, only white child in the remote Aboriginal community, far far away in lonely lonely woop woop land....' But there were other kids,

37

and it didn't feel remote; it was home. Do you want to go home?"

"Yeah."

"I wonder what she'll be like, when you get back."

"Dunno."

"What am I going to do when you go, you rotten foot-and-mouth disease?" She slung the green mango back at him. "I probably won't see you for donkey's years."

"You know my email address?"

"Remote_Man@hotmail.com."

"Well, *use* it!"

On his last evening, Ned and Ray watched a man down the road carry a TV out of the house and put it on a chair under a huge spreading tree. He joined together five extension cords and plugged it in; then the family and all the neighbors sat around watching TV, catching the slight evening breeze.

"Makes all our clutter seem silly, doesn't it?" said Ray.

Long ropes of birds were silhouetted across the sunset. They watched a hawk being chased by a small bird.

"What makes a hawk take notice of a little bird like that?" asked Ned.

"Beats me," said Ray. Then he put his strong arm around Ned's shoulders and added, "Because the little bird has guts."

They watched a flock of pelicans glide low over the billabong, then water-ski down onto the surface. Piles of pink clouds flowed over the escarpment. There was a dry storm in the distance, a flicker, then the far-off rumble of thunder.

Massachusetts

Ned arrived back in Melbourne as brown as a nut, wearing an outsize gray T-shirt with a red goanna screen-printed on the back. Agnes and Janet met him at the airport. Janet had lost more weight. It was like hugging a scarecrow.

"Hello, mate."

"Hi, stick."

"Good to see you, Ned." She drew back to look at him. "You've got a crinkle in your chin."

"So have you."

The exit doors of the airport slid aside, and they walked out into a freezing wind. Ned was shivering when they reached the truck, and by the time they got home he could feel a sore throat settling in.

After Wakwak, home was bleak and cold.

"I'm not going to school. I feel lousy."

It was a relief to put off the whole school scene, but he brooded because it was boring without TV. There was nothing to do. He was angry at everything.

Janet was keen to show him an e-mail from Chris in Tucson, Arizona. For the first time in ages he caught a note of excitement in her voice.

"I know it's crazy...."

Hi Jan

My mother lives in a town called Concord, in Massachusetts. She's inviting you to stay. Go! She has a big house, she's a great cook and loves kids. Honestly, it would be good for her too. And I know fall would be a real tonic.

"Go to America?" Ned was stunned.

"What do you think, hmm?" Janet asked anxiously.

Stay with some strange old lady in her house? No way.

"What's 'fall,' anyway?"

"Autumn. It's supposed to be very beautiful."

"What about school?"

"Maybe you could go to school in..."

"You're *joking*!" said Ned.

"No, no. It's nothing," said Janet. "It was just an idea."

That night, although she'd taken her medication, he heard her crying again.

I don't want to go to America. Massachusetts? Somebody just made that word up. Yeah, the Bee Gees. She's bad enough here. What would she be like in a strange place? She won't turn up the heater because it costs money, but tickets to America cost squillions! And how can you trust some old lady you've never met? If I went to school there, would I be in year seven when I came back?

He asked her straight-out at breakfast: "Do you want to go to Massachusetts?"

"No."

Her words didn't give him the answer. It was the fact she wouldn't look him in the eye.

Okay, Holdfast, start packing.

Kuza

I'b god a cold in da doze. The doc says I have to lighten up. So I'm lightening up okay? Laugh or I'll punch you.

Looks like we're going to invade America in a small-scale two-person sort of way.

FAX

Part of my visu form, filled in & posted after school yesterday. If he posted it how come he still has it? Well, after I slotted it with my passport in the yellow letter box, I told Mum some of my funny answers.
SHE FREAKS TOTALLY OUT!
(I seem to have that effect.)

I was just trying to brighten up their boring form-filled day. Don't I have to lighten-up? We go & wait by the mailbox. The postman turns up & we explain what a silly naughty boy I was & he gives it back.
MORAL: DO NOT JOKE WITH PASSPORTS OR VISAS. THOSE PEOPLE DO NOT HAVE A SENSE OF HUMOUR.

Mum wants to go. For the first time since the frying pan she's got back a bit of buzz. No one will be asking questions there & she has always wanted to spend fall in New England. It will be a **complete change.**
If one more person says **complete change** I will give their head a **complete change.**

Bernard down the street is going to look after Monty and Python, and the others should be okay till November.

The completion of...
regulations for the section of the Legal form... must be sta...
and the present and future status of the applicant must be made for each person regardless of age...
A separate and complete application must be made for each person regardless of age...

31 NOTE: THIS SECTION MUST BE READ AND COMPLETED IN FULL

☑ Yes ☐ No

- Have you or are you afflicted with a communicable disease, dangerous mental or physical disorder, or drug addiction? (31B3)......

A BAD CASE of of chewing gum addiction

- Are you seeking to enter the country to carry out violations of the export control regulations, or to conduct terrorist attacks?

☑ Yes ☐ No *Ba*

rockets in suitcases with gun running as a sid

- Do you belong to a group currently conducting subversive activities? (3) H4)

☑ Yes ☐ No

- Are you or have you ever been a prostitute or knowingly sold a restricted substance (drug) as classified by the Justice Administration. (3) G7l.....

☑ Yes ☐ No

yep definately. All the time. Want some thi

- ...ever been involved in the activities of the German
- ...Have you ever taken part in genocide?

☑ Yes ☐ No

whole heap of ants

☐ No

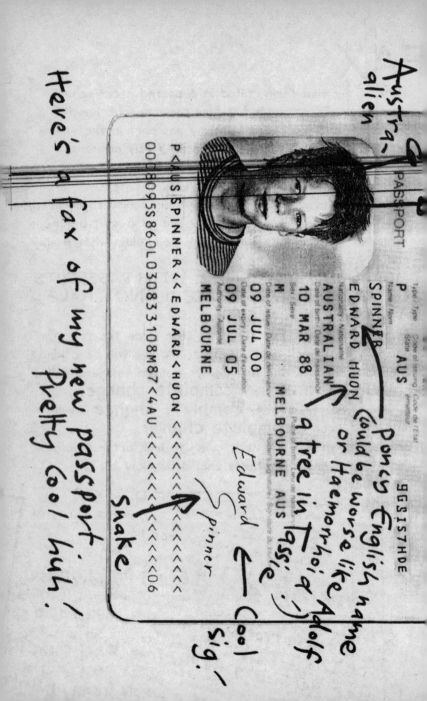

just I carry it with me everywhere in case some one has a heart attack and their dying words are...

I have...a "ticket...to...Disneyland...Can anyone...use...it...

She's going to look after me!

What about sitting in need?

he Governor-General of the Commonwealth of ustralia, being the representative in Australia of her Majesty Queen Elizabeth the Second, quests all those whom it may concern to allow e bearer to pass freely without let or hindrance and to afford him or her every assistance and otection of which he or she may stand in need.

```
 |_____      |
 |                                   \
 |_____    \__//
                                   \__/
```

*Typical Kate! What's this other thing I bookmarked? Oh
yeah, Macroalgae, the seaweed site...it runs like some game I
know.*

He scratched a bite on his wrist as he waited for the
screen to settle.

Enter code for Round Rock.

*Round Table! Yes! It's based on Dark Knights of the Round
Table. King? Not Alfred. Neptune! Members only area. Enter
profile and password. Yep. Second lead. A double code entry
like Dark Knights!*

He tapped in the answer then up came the heading—
The Kelp Room.

An empty forum. What's the point of it?

He left a message on the blank screen.

44

Martha B. Sudbury

Clang, clang, clang, clang...*TooOOoooooooWWOOoooooo!* The train whistled mournfully.

"Conquered!" shouted the conductor, sliding back the heavy inside door.

They waited nervously by the carriage door with all their bags, despite the sign saying *"Passengers are not permitted to ride in this vestibule."* The train had pulled out of one station before they could read its name, so they weren't taking any chances. Fear of missing their stop kept them awake all the way from Boston, forty minutes on the warm rocking train.

They stepped aside as the conductor slid open the outside door and lifted up a heavy patterned metal floor plate to reveal four steep steps to the ground. There was no platform. The passengers scrambled down.

Ned heaved their luggage to Janet, letting other passengers through between bags. They were heavy and the train was high.

Why did she bring so much stuff? Doesn't America have books on trees? All those winter clothes. Why is it so hot?

He was sweating like a pig. Their bags bumped to the ground.

"One, two, three, four, five..." Janet counted them for the ninth time.

Ned scanned the small crowd for a Martha B. Sudbury type of person.

"Last one." Ned jumped to the ground.

BANG! The conductor slammed down the metal floor

plate. Janet leapt as if it was a gunshot. The train snaked away and left them standing by the tracks.

Where's Martha B. Sudbury? Why didn't she meet us at the airport? Did she get Mum's message on the answering machine from the airport? Was it a proper message? Is Martha B. Sudbury some bizarre game on the Net? How long can this nightmare go on?

Ned's eyes felt like pink boiled onions, and his body didn't seem to belong to him any more.

Janet scrambled in her purse for change to phone Martha again. She peered at the strange coins. She dropped a couple. Then she dropped her purse. Ned wished he could just crawl under a rock.

They'll think she's on drugs. She is on drugs.

As he bent down to help her pick them up, they bumped heads. "Oww!" "OOoh!"

The last car pulling out of the now-deserted station parking lot slowed and the driver's window glided down. Then came the first American kindness.

"Where're ya goin'?" A man leaned out.

"Oh!" Janet straightened up. She had tears in her eyes.

"To find a phone," said Ned.

"You okay?" He peered at Janet. "Here, use my cell phone."

Ned called Martha again. The same message on the answering machine.

"You *sure* you're all right?"

"We were expecting a friend to meet us," faltered Janet, "but…we'll get ourselves there and…I'm sure we'll find a note…or something…."

The man didn't hesitate. "I'll drive you there."

46

Don't ever get into cars with strangers.

"I'll pop the trunk."

"Beg your pardon?"

The car boot lid flew up to reveal a cave the size of Ned's bedroom.

"I'm Bob, by the way."

Bob drove in a slow leisurely fashion and Ned's eyes began to close. The houses were nestled among trees twice their height, and squirrels darted away as they drove by.

Letter boxes with red levers, and Sesame Street fire hydrants, no fences... we're living in TVland—everyone's happy all the time....

"You're not from around here, are you?" Bob asked.

Ned dragged his eyes back open. "Melbourne. Australia."

"Oh my! How long did it take to get here?"

"About"—he stared at his watch trying to make sense of it—"twenty-nine hours."

"Well, you've arrived," said Bob heartily. "Two hundred and twelve Barrett's Pond Road."

He swung the car into the drive of an old two-story timber house surrounded by tall fir trees.

"Are you *sure* this is it?" said Bob. "Looks awful quiet. Check the number on the mailbox, Ned."

It was 212. Ned went round the doors and windows. Locked. Blinds drawn. No note. Nothing.

Next door, the garage was wide open but empty, just a little white dog in the front window yapping furiously. Janet sat in the backseat of Bob's car like a zombie.

"Is there a motel near here?" Ned asked.

"Well, the closest is"—Bob thought of their ragged

luggage—"expensive. There's another about a mile and a half along the highway that's cheaper."

"Would you take us there?" said Ned.

Janet collapsed onto the enormous bed, with no strength left to take off her shoes. Ned struggled with the knots, then pulled them from her feet. He fell onto the other bed.

Don't care how much this costs. All our bags are here and there's a lock on the door. We'll find Martha tomorrow. I can't do any more.

He was asleep in seconds.

What? Where am I? Can't see! Uhh…motel. Drink. Need a drink. So hot.

It was pitch black, he had a foul taste in his mouth, and his crumpled clothes were trying to strangle him.

"You awake, Ned?" came Janet's voice in the darkness.

"Yeah."

"There's a roll and cookies from the plane, and chocolate."

"Vegemite's in my pack."

Ned padded through the eerie sleeping parking lot, through the pools of light to the vending machine by the motel reception. He fed in the dollar bill. The can made a loud crash in the night as it dropped into the tray.

They ate a strange picnic by the light of Janet's bedside lamp. Two gray-faced, blinking refugees. They didn't talk much. The ceiling fan rattled and someone snored loudly next door. They shared the can of Strawberry Passion Awareness.

48

"We've got cable," said Ned, nodding at the TV.

"Don't."

Ned rummaged through his pack, then changed into his tiger boxer shorts. They'd never felt so good. Then he slept the sleep of the dead, sprawled across the huge bed like a letter half out of the envelope.

Bright sunlight streamed in every chink, and a note by the door said the cleaning staff had called.

"What time is it?" asked Janet.

Ned found his watch. "Half past two, but I don't know *where* it's half past two."

Janet lay staring at the ceiling.

"We're in some motel," said Ned, "on some highway in Massachusetts, near Concord pronounced Conquered...in America."

Clothes spewed from their opened cases. The remains of their late-night feed were strewn around as if birds had picked over a picnic. And it was *hot*.

See! It's not working out! He felt like shouting it, but what good would that do? Instead, he growled, "I'm starving," and pulled on some clothes.

He ran to the lobby, and half an hour later Papa Giuseppe's delivered a family-sized pizza with a huge bottle of Coke. Ned paid from Janet's purse. Janet stayed in bed, but she was hungry. When she fell asleep again, he slipped out.

Ned felt much better with food in his stomach, and the fresh air and sunshine lifted his spirits. From somewhere close by came the growl of a truck. He pushed through the fir trees behind the motel and suddenly found himself looking down on Bohager's Removals. It was a huge trucking company. The biggest moving vans Ned had ever seen shunted slowly in and out of its cavernous doors.

He settled under the trees to watch. Ever since the bust-up with Sean, he played a game in his head called Covert. Hidden beneath his everyday self was the hero, Remote Man, as tight as a coiled spring, ready for the attack which could come at any moment, in any form, from any direction. He could not prepare for it, but when the attack came, his reactions had to be whiplash fast.

Ned sat so quietly, the chipmunks, squirrels and birds weren't afraid. The squirrels seemed to hold the nuts with their wrists. They had a floating kind of run, and at the first hint of danger, leapt for a tree. The little chipmunks, with racing stripes down their sides, were as cute as living cartoons. He laughed as a squabbling pair chased each other, shrieking *"Chip chip chip chip chip!"* even though their cheeks were stuffed with nuts.

The shadows grew longer and several trucks returned. The drivers climbed down, walked stiffly to their cars and drove off.

Ned padded back to the motel room, where he lay at the end of his bed and watched the cartoon channel with the volume turned down. Janet was still asleep.

What if she doesn't get out of bed? She's going to love the motel bill.

No Car, Ma'am?

"We've been asleep for days." Janet was perched on the edge of her queen-sized bed, eating a pink iced donut from the motel lobby.

"This is what they have for breakfast. Want some?" she offered. "It's sickly sweet. Eat up. Breakfast is paid for with the room. I want you to eat at least three of them. And there's tea for you too." He grinned. She wanted him to eat iced donuts! But she was agitated.

"We have to find Martha. We can't stay here, it's too expensive. The money's slipping through our fingers like water."

"It can't be *that* expensive," said Ned. "Look at all the stains on the carpet."

"Well, it's cheap if you're American, but we're poor here, Ned."

"So? We're poor at home!"

"We're *much* poorer here."

Where are we going to go? Down a chipmunk hole?

Ned remembered the nightmare scene at the airport, when Martha wasn't there to meet them. It was a memory he'd rather forget. First the phone ate their quarters when they tried to call her, so Ned bought a phone card.

Janet reeled away from the phone in shock. "I left a message on her answering machine and I've used it all!"

"You can't have. That cost five bucks. What a rip-off!"

Janet stood there, blinking. People were watching them.

"We'll get there by ourselves," said Ned. "We'll catch a taxi to a train, then a taxi to her house."

"We can't afford it." Janet grew more agitated.

"What are we going to do?" yelled Ned. "Live here?"

WRONG! Oh no! There's the old wrinkle in the chin. Now she's going to lie down and cry in the middle of the airport!

He went for a cart that had just been left, then returning with it, he saw a man behind Janet about to steal one of their bags.

Ned dashed at him with the cart, and he melted into the crowd. Ned's legs were shaking as he stacked their luggage.

They kept on phoning Martha, but stopped leaving a message.

Ned called the days that followed "the walking time." No one else in the entire country walked, but they did.

"You can't have a car in your religion?" asked a friendly cleaner at the motel. Her name was Rosangela. She was Brazilian and had three kids who lived with her sister in Boston.

"No, we just haven't got one."

"Oh, okay," said Rosangela, but she looked perplexed.

Their first trek was to the supermarket, along Route 2. Cars streamed past at a frightening speed, so they kept as far from the highway as they could, sometimes knee-deep in grass by the trees.

But the highway sliced through the country like a canyon, so they had to cross it. They dashed to the center bar, climbed over, then waited for a break in the traffic to dash across the other lanes. It halved the journey but made them feel like runaways. People in passing cars gave them strange looks.

"Newsflash. Australian mother and son found shot in the back, walking in Americar. Police are still trying to locate their vehicle."

They discovered a shortcut past a row of empty houses near the prison. The prison was set at the intersection of five roads. They could see the guards in the high watchtowers. It was depressing, but the row of old wooden houses felt sinister, as if something was lurking in the overgrown gardens.

"They give me the creeps," said Janet, and she wouldn't go back that way.

The supermarket was a huge barn surrounded by a vast parking lot. They bought spicy chicken legs and rolls, sat on the seat outside and gobbled them. Then they went back inside and bought more.

"Paperorplastic, ma'am?" asked the supermarket attendant as they stood in the line with food for the next few days.

"Pardon?"

"Paperorplastic, ma'am?"

"He means do you want the shopping in a paper bag or a plastic bag?"

"Oh." Janet balked at the choice. "Um…well…plastic, no, *paper,* thanks."

Yes, we have a decision!

The assistant packed the groceries into a thick paper bag and put it in the shopping cart.

"I'll push it out for ya, ma'am."

"No, please don't," said Janet, flustered.

"No trouble, ma'am. I get paid to do it, ma'am. Take 'em to your car, ma'am."

"We haven't got one," said Ned.

"Pardon me?"

"We haven't got a car," Janet blurted out.

He blinked at her.

We're from another planet. We don't have a car.

"Well, ma'am, I'll push 'em to the edge of the lot for ya, ma'am."

"Thank you."

"My pleasure, ma'am."

"Wish you'd got plastic, Mam," said Ned as they trudged back through the long grass. "Excuse me, Mam, but paper doesn't have handles, Mam. Dumb choice, Mam."

"But paper rots, you little rotter!" said Janet with a grin.

Hey, we have a joke! Paper bags—miracle cure for depression.

From then on, Ned called her Mam.

Their second trek was to Martha's house. It took them forty-three minutes.

The sweat didn't evaporate, just ran down Ned's T-shirt.

"Looking for Martha?" called a neighbor, half-hidden by a hedge. "She's in Ohio. Her godson has chicken pox. I'm sorry, I don't know the phone number there, but she'll be back next week."

It was as simple as that.

Why didn't she let us know?

Martha's shed was stacked with old outdoor furniture, garden tools, skis, camping gear, bikes, a sled, canoes, all the equipment for adventure. And a tent.

Ned had an idea, the sort of idea Janet would have had before she crashed. It was going to be very embarrassing, but if they wanted to have enough money for a computer and e-mail, it was the best thing to do.

"Does this motel have e-mail, Rosangela?"

"Sure."

"Is it expensive to e-mail Australia?"

Rosangela winked. "After three o'clock, Mary on the desk will help you to send a quick one."

> **Kuza**
> Greetings from USA. We're here but Martha's not. She's coming back next week. But tell Helena we're surviving. We're staying in a motel with cable!!
> R M

While Janet slept in the late afternoon, Ned watched the moving company.

"What are you doin' up there with the squirrels?" called one of the drivers. "Why don't you hang with your friends?"

Does he think I'm a fruit bat?

"I'm here with my mother from Australia. She's on long service leave…" *from her head.*

"You like trucks?"

"Yeah, and cars. We're going to get a car."

"What sort?"

"I'd like a McLaren F1, I'd settle for a Dodge Viper, but it'll probably be, like, a Toyota Camry."

The man laughed. "I'm Gerry. Want a nickel tour of Bohager's?"

Ned ran back to the motel full of news about Bohager's, but as he pushed open the door, a piece of paper crinkled.

Janet rolled over drowsily and watched him read the note. "What is it?"

His face took on a stubborn look. He folded the note three times and jammed it into his pocket. "Nothing."

"No, what?"

"Pizza offer."

"We're not having pizza delivered again."

Sitting beside the vending machine with a can of Fruit Integration, he read Kate's e-mail again.

Just as well you're on the OTHER SIDE OF THE WORLD otherwise I would KILL YOU!!!!! DUMB IDIOT!!!
You know thECowboy? Who was so NOT interested in snakes? And you told him ALL about the Oenpelli python and eXACTLYwhere we saw it?
They camped near there.
Without a guide.
WELL, We've been back there FOUR times since and we haven't see the python again. Moses and some others are sure they took it. And YOU are the ratty RAT that RATTED on the python.

YOU didn't CARE.
%^*&^%*&^%*!!!!!!!
NOwPhilemon and Moses say I can't be trusted. RUinATOR!!
ANDthe Cowboy rang Dolobbo and bought your FAVOURITE small
skeleton X-ray snake picture. Seems he WAS very
interested in snakes. HHMM yes VERY INTERESTED!!!!!!
YOu're in America soFIND it and send it BACK!!!!

```
K        ) ) ) ) ) ( ( ( (
     ( ( ( (   U        U   ) ) ) )
        {      7       }
        (      ^      )
                ___
               I I
        = + = + = + = + =
```

PS Well, I suppose I'm glad you're still alive. A bit.

Ned had a tight burning feeling in his chest. It sounded bizarre that the Cowboy could have taken the python, but somehow he knew in his bones it was true. He'd read articles about wildlife smuggling from the Top End. There were landing strips all over the Northern Territory from World War II, and the Cowboy had a plane and everything.

Curse him! That beautiful python. It will be in Asia now, or America, in a heated cage. I didn't know that would happen. I did care. I do care. Jeez, I hate that man!

Ned could see the snake lying on the rock, but Australia seemed as distant as the moon just then. He felt bad about Monty and Python and his blue-tongues.

What if that boy, Bernard, doesn't care about them? And Kate? Still a friend?

A Real Meal

When Martha B. Sudbury returned home about breakfast time on Sunday, she found Chris's blue two-man tent erected on the grass in front of her house.

"Well, my goodness!"

Ned stuck out his head and looked up at a tall, older woman, plumpish, with a big behind and a wide smile.

"Martha B. Sudbury, I presume?"

"Good presuming! You must be Ned."

"And I'm Janet."

"Well, you weren't going to be anybody else," said Martha, absolutely beaming, as if she'd discovered something the fairies had left on her doorstep. The embarrassing moment Ned had been dreading didn't even happen.

"Smart idea," said Martha. "I don't have to clean the house now. Good little tent, isn't it? Were you eaten alive? The mosquitoes and flies here are murder. Guess I don't need to tell you. Well now, how about a cup of coffee, and some fresh cider for you, Ned?"

There was an envelope on the hall table. Ned recognized the Australian stamp and his mother's familiar handwriting. When he thought Martha wasn't looking, he unfolded the letter, and there, as plain as the nose on your face, was the wrong date—the clearest thing on the page of scrawl. Ned opened his mouth, but Martha gave him a sharp glance and he shut it. She never missed a beat.

"You're upstairs on the left," she said to Ned.

A room of his own, with a door! The windows looked down over a patch of lawn with a backdrop of tall trees. He hoped Janet had trees, because he wasn't going to swap. It felt so good bringing their stuff in from the tent and unpacking into drawers, and putting things where they would stay.

Martha looked at Australia on a map of the world. "Oh my, that is *such* a long way."

"We lost a day."

"Oh, if I kept flying backward, would I get younger?" said Martha.

"Corny." Ned grinned.

"You laughed," said Martha.

Ned came across his pencil case with the large S he'd scratched on the lid. They expected him to go to school when it started in early September. He threw it in the back of the bottom drawer and forced the dreaded thought from his mind.

Janet was unpacking her books and papers onto shelves in Chris's old room.

"I can see why you call her Ma'am," said Martha, tapping Janet's name on the cover of a book. "This lady deserves respect!"

There were photos all through Martha's house, black-and-white and colored: photos of people in canoes, on bikes or horses, skiing down slopes, climbing out of tents, standing on mountains. It was strange to think that this large house had been home base for all these adventures. Now it was occupied by one getting-old woman.

Ned's favorite photo was of an expedition about to begin. A family in high spirits, including a boy with a bucket on his head, stood proudly at the front of the house by a massive black DeSoto. Bags were tied to the running board, and lashed on top of the car was a huge canoe.

"Can you find me?" said Martha.

Ned searched. "No. Where?"

She pointed to the head of a little girl in the back window of the car. "Ready to go!"

The sitting room was furnished with three large, beaten-up, comfortable chairs and a couch, mumbling to each other like toothless old people. There was a wooden cupboard, a low wooden table, a worn rust-colored Indian rug and a rocking chair, but no sign of a TV.

A door under the stairs led down to the basement, which contained the furnace. The furnace was like a dragon harnessed beneath the house, providing hot water and heating in winter though a system of pipes.

In front of the bathroom sink was an antique painting of a duck.

"I don't do mirrors," said Martha.

"Do you do TV?" asked Ned.

"Sometimes. It's in a cupboard."

They were settling in well, but on Martha's terms.

"It's her house, you know," said Janet.

"We have to talk to her about a computer and e-mail," said Ned. "She doesn't like computers much, which is funny because she fixes things. She's got a drill and an orbital sander. She's not a technophobe."

"Ned!" Martha called from downstairs.

The back of the kitchen door was marked with lots of lines and names and dates.

"I'll use blue for you. Take off your shoes."

Ned stood against the door, and Martha marked his height and wrote the date beside it.

"Now, grow!" she said. "Out and up, okay?"

60

No meal ever tasted as good as dinner that night. The potatoes were creamy with melted butter, and the Cajun fried chicken was doused in rich gravy. Even the beans weren't bad.

Ned told Martha about his lizards; then Martha told them about the pet raccoon she had as a girl, growing up on a farm in Ohio. "I called him Walter. I used to dress him up. I've got photos of him somewhere."

There was apple pie and ice cream for dessert.

"We're coming up to apple time. You'd better get used to apples."

It was still hot at ten o'clock that night. Ned lay on the bed with his eyes open, and in his head he e-mailed Kate. He tried to think of how to say sorry for the python. He told her what they had for dinner and about Martha's raccoon and her couch and her fridge. He finished up: *This place feels more like home than home.*

In the motel, the darkness had seemed hot and thick, in the tent it felt heavy, but here it settled softly around him.

11

Into the Forest

As Ned helped himself to breakfast next morning, he overheard Martha on the phone. She was trying to find another boy his age, but they were all away at summer camp or on vacation with their families.

Phew! Lucky escape.

Ned liked Martha, but she sure was bossy.

"I'm going out back," he yelled to Janet.

Ned pushed his way through the green curtain of leaves at the bottom of the lawn and found himself in the forest. He stepped so suddenly from the suburban to the wild, it was like a magician's trick. He laughed out loud. It felt secret, exhilarating and unreal, like the beginning of a story.

He climbed downhill, in a straight line from the house, struggling through prickles and bending back branches, then the undergrowth opened out. It was a path—not used much, but definitely a path. He found a stick and scratched an arrow pointing to Martha's house, then chose to go left.

The path twisted through the trees up a short hill, then down to a dry creek with rocks that were obviously stepping stones when the creek was flowing. He hopped nimbly across. It was like hopping around rocky headlands of beaches back home.

Easy to get lost here. Need landmarks... a rock like a turtle back... step over tree trunk... moss in the shape of a hat....

He stopped and listened.

Chickadees and finches... a squirrel in a tree some-

where…the train whistle from West Concord.

He came to another creek where a little waterfall trickled into a pool. Ned kicked over a rock, and there was a creature he'd never seen before, except in books—a salamander. Shaped like a lizard, black, dotted with bright yellow spots, it lay in his hand like a little wet rubber toy.

"You're a slow one, not like the skinks back home." He slipped it back under the rock.

The path ran along beside a stone wall, not rough but not neat either. It blended in so well it might almost have been a natural part of the forest.

Man-made. Not high enough to keep in animals. Probably a boundary. Where it catches the sun, I find a snake….

Ned lifted a large flat rock and dropped it with a thud, jumping to one side so it missed his foot.

A pigeon took off and suddenly a boy crashed out of the undergrowth, like an ambush. "Freakin' woodchucks! You scared off my *bear*!" His arms beat furiously in an oversize shirt, like ragged wings. "Dang dang dang nabbit! I think I nearly saw him. I heard him, that's for sure. Drat! Drat! Double drat!" He glared at Ned through his black-rimmed glasses. "It was the bear for *sure*."

He was roughly the same age, a little taller and much wider, with scratches on his legs and a green Band-Aid on one hand. He looked about to begin another comic-book tirade when a formation of geese interrupted, honking and cackling loudly overhead. Their wings beat *sh sh sh sh sh.*

Everything's beating its wings at me!

"What are you doing here, in the whole of tarnation?" asked the kid.

"Looking for snakes and lizards," said Ned.

"You won't find any," said the boy, "I've only ever seen black snakes down by Concord Meadow, like licorice all twisted round. Once. And I know these woods."

"I found a salamander."

"Oh, plenty of them," said the boy. "I've got three corn-snakes."

Ned stared at him.

"You don't say much, do you? I'm after the bear. He's around here somewhere. Where are you from?"

"Australia."

"Cool. I live in Acton."

"Aren't bears dangerous?"

"Yep," said the kid. "Want to help me find him?"

"Yes."

"Well, stop dropping rocks." He suddenly looked at his watch. "Shoot! Gotta go. You know the dry stream?"

"Yes."

"Meet you there at two o'clock?" He flapped off up the track, then paused at a bend to yell back, "What's your name?"

"Ned."

"I'm Rocky."

Like something from Alice in Wonderland...he jumps out and runs off. Some people treat you as if you're a really good friend, then you never see them again. A bear. As if.

"Did you go into the woods?" Martha asked at lunch. "Now you be careful. There's a bear round here somewhere. I just read about it in the paper."

So the bear is real!

Ned hurried back to the stream before two o'clock, only to find a scrap of yellow paper anchored by a stone, fluttering in the breeze.

> Have to go to the dentist. See you around.
>
> Rocky

He is from Alice in Wonderland.

12

All@once

Ned went to the orientation afternoon at Concord Junior High with his face set in the snake mask. No one spoke to him, and he spoke to no one. When he came home, he was sullen and took off into the woods.

Everything about school was foul.

On Thursday, Janet combed through *The Acton Beacon*, the *Concord Journal* and the *Carlisle Mosquito*, drawing red rings around used cars, computers and yard sales. She was determined to find a car. "To do anything in this place, you need a car."

"Now, the bus list's out today," Martha said to Ned. "Let's see which one you're on." She was annoyingly cheerful. "Here we are, bus number fourteen, 6:45 A.M."

"6:45 A.M.? No way!"

"Fraid so," said Martha in her no-nonsense voice.

"How will I wake up?"

"Same way other kids do." She dug out Chris's old alarm clock from the basement. It was shaped like a brick, with digital numbers two inches high and an alarm like a repeating sonic boom.

Ned made the bus that first morning with five minutes to spare and money in his pocket to buy lunch. As they drew closer to the school, the road was crowded with a swarm of buses, like chunky square yellow bees buzzing back to the hive.

At lunchtime, Ned walked out among the tables in the cafeteria, sure that everyone was watching him. He sat in a corner facing the wall, ate his slice of pizza and thought of Kate.

He finished lunch as soon as he could and went to the library, where he hung around the desk.

"Need help?" The librarian was a large woman with a friendly face.

Ned plucked up courage. "Can you send e-mail from here?"

"You're the Australian boy, aren't you?"

"Yes."

"Slip into my office. I'm feeling in a good mood."

Kuza

I am honestly sorry about the Oenpelli python. I didn't know that would happen.

That's all I can say.

But I think about it a lot.

If it makes you feel any better, my life isn't so great.

Today is my first day of school. Up at 5:45am! I was so worried I wouldn't wake up I didn't sleep all last night.

Missing school is much more big deal than in Australia.

I guess if they give you more than two months summer holiday they want you to work. We've got homework already.

No uniform so I didn't know what to wear. I feel like a dag.

Everyone is so sure of themselves and the girls are flirty.

Grey metal lockers. long & skinny with a hook for your coat in winter. kids put pics up inside with magnets.

Kids flunk if they don't get good enough grades. I won't be here long enough to flunk. I'm flunking at friends though.

If I find the python I'll bring it back alive and if I find the Cowboy I'll bring him back dead

Been nice talking to you. You have a nice day now.

Remote Man

Janet and Martha were desperate to know every detail of his day.

"Oh, come on, Ned, how *was* it?"

"Livable."

"Well, take a look at this, Old Ned Nod." He hadn't heard that name for ages—Janet was happy about something.

The living room was strewn with boxes. An instruction manual lay open on the floor by the TV.

"We're on-line."

"You're *kidding*!"

Janet flourished her arms like a game show host. "Ta-dah! WebTV. I bought it for Martha. She's already sent an e-mail to Chris."

Martha, suddenly the expert, bustled in from the kitchen. "Let me show you."

She plomped herself between them on the old couch, turned the TV to channel 4, turned on the VCR, pressed power on her keyboard, and a light came on in the small black box above the TV.

"Internet terminal through the phone line. How do you pay?"

Martha pulled a haggard face. "We typed my credit card details onto the TV screen."

"You're not comfortable with this?" twanged Ned in an American accent.

"No."

"Who connected it?"

"We did, this afternoon," said Martha proudly.

"Martha, you little space cadet!" said Ned. "Two problems. You can't print out, and it's in the living room."

"Tough," said Martha.

"I can think of another problem," said Janet.

"What?"

"Homework."

She was *definitely* starting to act normal.

While Martha and Janet went for a walk, Ned gave himself his own user name and checked out the chat rooms and games. There they were, just as they had been at home. He didn't even need the keyboard—he could do it all via the remote, lying on the couch.

Remote Man flies again!

Kuza
COMMUNICATIONS BREAKTHROUGH!!!!!
We have email!!!!!!!!!!!!!!!!!!!

```
Y       Y    EEEEEEEE    sSSSSS    I  I  I
 Y     Y     E           S         I  I  I
  Y   Y      EEEE        SSSSSs    I  I  I
   Y         E                 S   I  I  I
   Y         EEEEEEEE    SSSSSs    o  o  o
```

As you can see I am V pleased.

Martha is bossy, but pretty cool. She and Mum talk about trees. This place is exceptionally tree-infested, with a lot of ponds. Fall hasn't started falling. It's hot.

I met an oddbod kid called Rocky. He was looking for a bear in the woods. Like a fairy story hey?. A bear!

Haven't found any snakes (or the python) but plenty of mosquitoes. Martha's back porch is screened off. like being in a meat safe. we're the meat.

Concord (Conquered!!!!!) is historic & touristic picture-book town, made of fresh painted two story doll's houses, decorated with picture banners & American flags & basketball rings. In the middle of Concord there's an EXCELLENT toy shop & library withstatues & oil paintings.

BUT strangely

Right on Route 2 is a whacking great prison.

Tell Helena, Mum—Mam (because a supermarket packer called her Ma'am about fifty times)—has actually made a few decisions & is acting more normal every day, like nagging about home-work. (How normal can you get!)She has a big bedroom & an office where she can work if she feels like it. She and Martha go wakling all the time.

Write to me NOW! Right NOW! Write!!! NOW!!!!!

Looking forward to hearing from you in case you hadn't guessed.

Remote Man

When the walkers returned, Ned entered into the WebTV all of Martha's friends' and relatives' e-mail addresses and showed her how to bookmark sites.

Martha was impressed. "Wow, Speedy, you'll get blisters!"

After his sleepless night and jam-packed day, Ned was exhausted. Janet went up to say good night.

"It's working out," she said seriously, settling on the edge of his bed.

"Yeah, WebTV is cool." Ned lay with his eyes shut, like a talking corpse. "But don't you need a computer for work?"

"Martha's niece is lending me an old Mac laptop. WebTV is good, Ned, but Martha can't receive phone calls when it's on. You take a turn last thing before bed. I'll try to get back to the early mornings."

"Do you think you can?"

She sighed. "You know the Shaker quilt on my bed? Well, making my bed has become a ritual. I smooth the quilt over the top and I tell myself it's sealed."

"You're getting better."

She smiled wistfully. "Oh, sometimes I long to climb back in."

"Oops!" Ned's eyes snapped open. "Nearly forgot. I've got a surprise for you too." He stumbled from the bed, found the tissue in his jeans pocket and gave it to her.

Janet unfolded it.

"What's the tooth fairy's exchange rate?" asked Ned.

There was the old wrinkle in the chin.

She looked at him tenderly. "Night, sweet Ned."

"Night, Mam."

Bear Hunt

"Hi, Ned!" It was the boy, Rocky, as bright and chirpy as if they'd been buddies for fifty years. He bounced toward Ned, whipping overhanging leaves with a stick, his shirtfronts flapping either side of his ample stomach.

"Found any snakes yet?" He grinned.

Ned shook his head. "Found the bear?"

"Nope. Welcome to the Totally Unsuccessful Bear and Snake Hunters' Club. But I know where it is this time."

He fished in his pocket for chewing gum and offered some to Ned. "I'm going up beyond First Stream. Wanna come?"

"First Stream?" said Ned.

"This is Second Stream. First Stream's got the stepping rocks."

He was just like a cartoon character.

Bet a light bulb pings on over his head when he gets a good idea.

Rocky set off at a fast clip, with Ned following. He walked with his arms out from his sides as if he was wading, and his shirt was always flapping. He stopped along the way to point things out; Ned's self-appointed guide.

"See that? That's a squirrel's drey. Kind of like a summer house for them. And there's where they've buried acorns. Sometimes they bury 'em and forget 'em and they grow into oaks. And smell that?"

"Sure do."

"Skunk. Lucky it's a fair way off."

My first skunk!

They crossed First Stream and slowed down. "I think the bear's here somewhere."

They left the path and scrambled through the undergrowth as quietly as they could, which wasn't quiet at all, then sat silently for some time beneath a black oak and listened.

"If he gets dangerous," whispered Rocky, "I'll hit him on the snout." He shook his stick, then he handed Ned a couple of party poppers. "And these should frighten him off. Never get between a bear and its young or a bear and its food."

"Can they run?"

"Fast. They can hit thirty miles an hour. And their sight is poor, but their sense of smell is amazing."

That was the first of many times Rocky led the bear hunt. They always set out with Rocky saying cheerfully, "I know where he is this time."

The Rockys

"I'm going to meet Rocky's snakes and his family," said Ned.

"I don't like you in the woods with a bear around," said Janet.

"It's okay, Mam, it's like with snakes back home—you just watch out."

Bears are much more dangerous.

"And a word of advice," said Martha.

Now what?

"They call it New England reserve," said Martha. "Folks can be a bit standoffish, so don't be upset if they aren't very friendly, it's just their way."

Rocky's mother, Vivian, wasn't home. She had an important government job in Boston and drove home late from the station each evening. Rocky's dad, Dave, was home. He worked at Acton Motors and ran the house. They ate a lot of pancakes.

"This is Ned from Melbourne," said Rocky.

"Not another Ned from Melbourne!" exclaimed Dave.

"Who was the other one?" said Rocky.

"The first film ever made was *Ned Kelly*, shot in Melbourne. You've got a lot to answer for, Ned."

"This is my sister, Abigail," said Rocky.

"I'm adopted," said Abigail.

She had smooth dark brown skin and tight black curls. She was tough, nine, and not pretty.

"She's a pain in the everywhere," said Rocky.

Abigail kicked him in the leg.

"See what I mean."

"I can ice-skate," Abigail informed Ned. "On my first lesson I fell over backwards and got concussion."

"Knocked clean out cold learning how to bow," laughed Rocky.

Abigail was fanatical about making videos and knew every trick in the camera: fades in and out, vignettes, star filter, everything. She was clever.

Abigail had two close friends, Kari and Jade. Rocky called them the Munchkateers. They collected bottles and cans, spending the refunds on videotapes. They loved watching themselves. Ned saw their video of Rocky snoring, Kari's feet in her new shoes, and Sleeping Beauty with Kari's dog as the prince. For the wake-up kiss, the dog gave Sleeping Beauty a slobbery lick right on the lips. Abigail had the knack of filming the weirdest details. Even Rocky had to admit that most of what they did was funny.

Abigail, Kari and Jade thought Ned was cute.

"Do you have a kangaroo?"

"No."

"What's it like in Australia?"

"Well, people breathe air and they eat food."

"Have you ever patted a koala?"

"No."

"Do you go surfing?"

"Do you know Crocodile Dundee?"

Then the questions ran out, because that was all they knew about Australia.

Rocky's house was a curious mixture of order, chaos, and noise. A huge two-door refrigerator with a temperamental ice dispenser added to the clatter. When Ned helped himself to ice, it made Titanic ice-grinding noises. The cubes shot into Ned's water, splashing the front of the fridge, the floor and Ned's shorts.

"Big mistake," said Rocky. "Ice *first*."

Life seemed to revolve around the refrigerator. The doors were a mass of stickers and magnets. *"Man belongs to Earth, Earth does not belong to man."*

When its big doors swung open, the lights went on in a fabulous mini supermarket jammed with jars and packets, open and ripped, all colorful and tempting.

"Why are these socks in the freezer?" yelled Dave.

"They're wintering over. There's seeds in 'em. They're going to grow," protested Abigail.

"They can winter over outside."

"No, they need total permafrost," pleaded Abigail.

"Oh, frogs legs they do." Dave slammed the freezer door, but Ned noticed a week later, when Rocky reached in for ice pops, the socks were still in the freezer.

There was an empty mug by the phone that said *"Go ahead, steal my pens. None of them work anyway."* It was that sort of a place.

"Where do you keep your snakes?" Ned asked.

"In my room."

"I've got a guinea pig called Fuzzwad," said Abigail, "and Squeek, a mouse I saved from being snake food."

Rocky's room was a mess. There was a pinboard covered with drawings of Warhammer figures, a bookcase with books on inventions, wildlife, kites and reptiles, and a snake sculpture that Rocky had made in woodwork, which was a branch in the shape of a snake, sanded smooth and painted.

Rocky took the lid off a large glass case and reached into

a black plastic cave. "There's an electric heat pad underneath here. It's their warm spot."

He gently lifted out his snakes.

"This is Sneaky, because he always sneaks up your sleeve, he's a male, and this is Diabolo, because it was my favorite word when I got him, and this is Buckeye. I had an albino, Blizzard, but when we went on vacation the people who were looking after him lost him."

The cornsnakes were elegant, slender and delicately patterned.

"They're beautiful," said Ned. "My lizards are ockers compared to them."

"What's an ocker?"

"A rough Aussie bloke with a beer gut."

Ned felt a pang of longing for his lizards; they were such characters. He hoped they were getting some snails for treats.

Ned and Rocky watched the snakes slither over Rocky's comforter. Sneaky wanted to slide under the pillow and down to the floor. Ned gently lifted him back every time he got to the pillow.

"Dinnertime," said Rocky. "I give them each a mouse twice a week."

"Where are the mice?"

"In the basement."

They put the snakes back in the glass case; then Ned followed Rocky down the stairs into the darkness.

"We don't have basements in Australia," said Ned.

"How can you live without a basement?" said Rocky.

The lights flickered on in the large windowless room. In the center stood an enormous table littered with electronic and mechanical parts. Ned recognized pieces of a phone, a clock, a camera, and circuit boards from computers.

"Cool! What do you do with this stuff?"

"I take 'em apart to see how they work," said Rocky.

"Can you put them back together?"

"Sometimes. That's why they call me Rocky. You know, Rocky Raccoon? Raccoons are neat with their hands."

Ned went to unscrew a solenoid.

"You're tightening it," said Rocky. "Righty tighty, leftie loosie. Doesn't your dad teach you stuff?"

Ned said nothing.

"Gotta feed the snakes," said Rocky quickly.

Rocky took three frozen teenage mice from a pack in the freezer.

"Fuzzies. I used to feed 'em live mice, but Abigail made such a fuss. She kept saving their lives. Dad was going to stop the fight by getting rid of my snakes; then I read in a magazine that live mice might scratch your snake anyway, so I started buying these. Abigail won't open this freezer."

Rocky put the small stiff bodies into a bowl of hot water.

"Mice on Ice. You have to defrost 'em."

Upstairs in his bedroom again, Rocky laid Diabolo on the carpet and put down a mouse. "You won't see him get it. It's faster than the eye can see. There! You see that? Bet you didn't! Now come on, Sneaky, old fella. When he's frightened, he shakes his tail against the side of the tank like he's going to attack. They're hungry. See how they act exhausted. They'll go slow after eating too. They can climb. Buckeye got out once and we couldn't find him."

Ned examined the scales under the snake's chin. "I think Buckeye's a female."

78

"Yeah?"

"And she's bigger. Females are generally larger."

Rocky was impressed. "Tell me about your reptile career."

"Well, it began when I was five," said Ned. "I saw a snake go down a hole and Mam says I sat beside the hole for an hour waiting for it to come out again. Then a herpetologist came to school camp with his snakes and lizards and I loved the feeling of them. I've had about thirty-five lizards."

"Where do you keep them?"

"Dad and I built a cage over my old sandbox. It's big enough to walk around in. Mam helped me plant native grasses and bushes; then we dragged back rocks and rotting branches and curls of bark from the country. Now it's so overgrown you can't see the wire netting. It's like real bush."

"Cool."

"I know they're happy because they keep having babies. When I left, there were twelve blue-tongues and two stumpy-tails."

"What do you do with all the young ones?"

"Take them to the zoo. And I have two Cunningham skinks in my bedroom, Monty and Python. Monty was pregnant when I left. People say lizards don't have any personality, but they sure do. I love the way the little ones flatten themselves on the rock under the light."

They talked for ages, about deaths and escapes, personalities and injuries, varieties and characteristics. Ned had never enjoyed a conversation so much. Then, sitting on the floor watching the cornsnakes, Ned told Rocky the whole sorry story of the Oenpelli python.

When Ned got home, the phone rang.

"Ned, it's for you," said Martha, surprised.

"Hi. It's Rocky. There's a thing about iguanas on TV tonight."

Ned bounded upstairs to his room. He didn't recognize the feeling at the time, but it was a creeping happiness. School was hard. He had homework—to memorize all the states of America. He didn't have a computer and he couldn't watch much TV, yet life was okay.

Wonder if Rocky's seen a rattlesnake?

"I don't think we need to worry about New England reserve," said Janet.

15

Kuza's Clue

Ned and Rocky were slurping up big bowls of noodles after another unsuccessful bear hunt, when Ned noticed the little red light flick on Martha's WebTV.

"We've got a fish on the line!"

> Ned Ned Ned, get off the sled.
> Use your head. That's what I said.
> I've got a thread. (It's me in case you haven't guessed.)
> A CLUE For YOU
> to DO (something)   ((((((((((( )))))))))))
> I can't be there   ((((((^ ^))))))))
> BO HO   ((((((7))))))))
> Boo Hoo   (^)
> BOO OOOO HOO   I I

"Is she like this in real life?" asked Rocky.

"Worse," said Ned, scrolling down the message.

> WELL
> eRemmber the Cowboy rang up & bought the X ray snake
> skeleton paintg. Your fave?
> WELL. He had it SENT .
> WELL. I snicked into the office and chicked out the order book
> and this iw what I foung. hard to REad. An address? Rock, get off
> your clock. What it all means? Huh?
> 40W72#2NYNY 10023
> ??
> GOOD LUCKY ROK and NED and BEAR

"Tallyho the *python!*" whooped Ned.

"That's an address in the Big Apple," said Rocky. "You can write to them."

"*Write?*" said Ned, like a dog that's just caught the scent. "No, we go there."

"Go there?" Rocky scratched his head. "Now one moment, Edward. That's a big bad city. The olds aren't going to say, 'Sure, honey bunch, you can go to New York. Here's a wad of money, have a good time.'"

Ned's mind raced, his knee jigged. "When you want something very badly, what do you do?"

"I asked for a snake every day for a year," said Rocky.

"Save up and pay half? Impossible. I'm not getting an allowance."

"Abigail pestered nonstop to get to *Disney on Ice*, but she risked death because the *olds* were ready to kill her."

"Did she go?"

"Yep."

Under the shelves of *National Geographic*s they found Martha's travel books. The guide to New York was quite worn and had a fold-out map.

"Where's West 72?" said Rocky. "Statue of Liberty. Skyscrapers, skyscrapers, King Kong. 42nd."

"No street names?" said Ned, puzzled.

"Numbers in New York, Edward, numbers. 50th, 59th, Upper West Side. It's round here somewhere."

"What's that empty bit?"

"Big park. Central Park. What's number 32 on the map? What's that?"

"Strawberry Fields."

"What's Strawberry Fields? Look it up."

Ned read aloud. "'Strawberry Fields is a part of Central Park that Yoko Ono had transformed in memory of her murdered husband, Beatle singer/songwriter John Lennon. It is the part of the park closest to the Dakota Building on the Upper West Side, where the Lennons lived.'"

"Anything else? Educational wins bonus points. Anything educational?"

"What's 33?"

A wide smile spread across Rocky's large face. "Pay dirt, my Australian friend! The Natural History Museum!"

"I don't *believe* it," said Ned. "I *want* to go there! I actually *do* want to go there! It's got a fantastic collection of dinosaur skeletons."

"What if we all go to New York and we have to drag around with the Munchkateers and don't even get near 40W72#2?" said Rocky.

"What if, what if, what if!" said Ned.

> **Kuza**
> It is definitely an address on the west side of the island of Manhattan New York. Maybe the Cowboy's apartment?
> We are now desperate to see dinosaur bones in the Natural History museum which is close to 40W72.
> What name did he send it to? HOw did the Cowboy pay? Does Ray know his name?
> A lead on the python. A bear in the woods

We're goin' huntin'!
Remote Man
PS
Tell Helena, Mam's reading a book! about Shakers, not pepper shakers—a religious mob who specialize in furniture but they're dying out because they don't believe in having children.
Martha's taking her to a Shaker museum at a place called Fruitlands. No comment.
PPS
Rocky lives on the north side of First Stream, we live on the south. I can see his bedroom light through the trees. We signal to each other with our lights—like Paul Revere
one quick flash — MEET YOU AT 1ST STREAM
one long flash — okay
Two flashes — 2nd STREAM
Three flashes — COME OVER HERE
Four flashes — HAVE TO STAY HOME
PPPS
I have to learn all the states of America. There's 50 of 'em! Groan.
PPPPS
Fall is falling. Some trees are so red they look like they're burning.

"Mam, there's an *awesome* exhibition of dinosaur bones at the Natural History Museum in New York," Ned announced. "Can we go?"

At the very same moment, on the other side of First Stream, Rocky was saying, "Dad, there's this brilliant dinosaur exhibition at the Museum of Natural History in New York, and we want to go by ourselves, not with a hundred other people. Cool?"

Operation NY NY was under way.

16

Black Bear

"The bear doesn't exist," moaned Ned as they thrashed their way back to the track on Nashoba Brook.

"Shhh! *Zounds!* What's that racket?"

Wraarf! Wraarf! Wraarf! Wraarf! Rraaaww!

"Dogs!"

"Someone's escaped from the prison!"

Their eyes met.

"Run!" said Ned.

"Which way?"

But Ned was already racing toward the commotion. Breathless, they stopped at the top of a rise where they could see down the track. In a thicket by the path, two hunting dogs leapt frantically at the trunk of a huge black pine. They were snapping and snarling in a frenzy. The dogs were heavy, with bullish heads, savage teeth and strong thickset legs.

"Whoa! Those dogs work out at the gym!" said Rocky. "No pattin' those fellas. Is it a raccoon?"

Ned stepped back and craned his neck, trying to see. He could just make out a dark patch through the leaves. Suddenly his jaw dropped.

"Rock, you're not going to believe this."

"What?"

"The *bear!*"

"*What?*"

"They've treed the bear!"

"I *don't* believe it. Where?"

"See, about twelve feet up. And there's another black lump. Look higher!"

"*A cub!*" Rocky squeaked.

"A cub!"

"They usually have two. Is there another?"

"Yes."

"Zounds! This I can't *believe!*" Rocky was over the moon.

The bear stared calmly down at them, through the branches. She was sitting comfortably, and higher up, looking for all the world like cuddly soft toys, were her two cubs.

Ned was determined not to share the bears with the owner of these dogs. He remembered what Kate had told him to do with the vicious camp dogs in Wakwak. Yelling like a banshee, flailing his stick and pelting rocks, he advanced. A stone struck the bigger dog, and he sprang around snarling and snapping, but Ned's stick was mid-swing and it made a good whistling noise.

"Get away from our bears!" yelled Rocky.

The dogs ran off, snarling and barking.

"Phew!"

Rocky still could hardly believe it. "We *found* the *bear!*"

"And the rest!"

They pushed through the bushes, trying to find the best spot to watch them.

"Wish we had Dad's binoculars. I'm going to run back and get them and tell the others."

"No," said Ned.

"Oh, *come* on, Ned, just our families. Besides we *need* Dad's binoculars."

Rocky returned half an hour later with Janet, Martha,

Abigail, Dave and the binoculars. Janet and Martha met Dave and Abigail for the first time.

"Congratulations, bear hunters. Not just one but *three* bears."

"And up a tree on display!"

They made a happy group, laughing and talking about the bears and taking turns with the binoculars.

"Oh, look at the cubs! *They're adorable!* I *love* them!" drooled Abigail. "I want one. Look at their little tufty ears and their long royal noses. Oh, he's scratching. Ohh!" She was melting. "I want to take him home."

"Just as well the other Munchkateers aren't here," said Rocky. "They'd levitate in mass adoration."

"Well, boys, a fine bear in the prime of life," said Dave.

"Look at the sheen on that coat," said Martha.

"Why didn't the newspaper say about the cubs?" said Abigail.

"She probably had them hidden," said Janet.

"We're going back now," said Dave to Rocky and Ned, "but if that bear moves one branch down that tree, you come home instantly. It's okay while she's up there, but on the ground she's dangerous."

"We're fine," said Rocky.

"Yes, but you like her so much, you'd let her eat your arm," said Abigail.

"Don't tell anyone, will you?" said Ned. "We don't want the place swarming with bear freaks. Promise? You especially, Abigail. Swear?"

"If I tell about the bears, I'll chop my own head off," said Abigail.

Everyone promised and the others trooped back up the

track, leaving Ned and Rocky to watch through the binoculars. The bear looked straight down her long, aristocratic nose into Ned's eyes. After the scare with the dogs, she seemed quite happy to sit in the tree until things quietened down. They watched her for ages, and finally Rocky's stomach rumbled loudly.

"Yeah," sighed Ned. "We'd better go."

"We'll find her again, easy," said Rocky. "Oh, and I forgot to tell you, Edward, if a bear is chasing you, don't go up a tree; they can climb."

"Yeah, right."

But Ned told someone else about the bear—a safe someone. In the longest e-mail he'd ever written, Ned told Kate everything. It was late when he typed the last bit.

> Feels like I know the forest now. I've sort of earned it, like a badge. It's not the same as the bush, but I'm not a total stranger. Rocky and I searched for that bear for so long—feels like she made us friends. She's our bear. Looked us in the eye.
> And then the others came, Abigail, Martha & Mam—it's like we're all friends now. Real friends.

Bit soppy? Delete? Nah. She'll understand.
He hit send, and went to bed.

17

Photographer

Ned went on another bear hunt, on the Net. For the first time he was really interested in something other than a reptile.

Cubs born mid-winter while hibernating in her den…half a kilo! Gee, that's small.

After the first sighting, Ned and Rocky lost the bears. They searched in vain for over a week, then found them again, by chance, in a remote part of the forest. They heard a strange humming noise and went looking for its source. It turned out to be the cubs singing a happy sort of hum as they drank from their mother. This secluded spot was inaccessible except by scrambling through briars along a stone wall.

The bear knew they were watching, but the only time she showed concern was when Rocky laughed aloud at one of the cubs stealing an acorn from a squirrel. With a snort she took a couple of steps in their direction, her ruff bristling, ears back. The boys were scared and quickly wriggled backward along the wall, their legs a mass of bruises.

They watched the cubs learning to climb, digging their claws into the tree's bark, then sliding down the trunk, using their claws as brakes. They seemed to eat anything: insects, roots, berries, grubs, grass. They even saw one chewing on a dead bird. Ned had read a description of cubs as "little black hooligans." It was true.

That Saturday morning, Rocky's bedroom light flashed furiously. Ned found Rocky dancing a shirt-flapping jitterbug at First Stream.

"A wildlife photographer wants to take photos of the bears for a magazine. He'll give us a hundred bucks if we tell him where they are."

Ned was suspicious. "Where'd you meet him?"

"In the woods."

"Which magazine?"

Rocky shrugged. "A hundred American bucks, Ned. That's a trip to New York!"

Ned wasn't convinced.

"A photo," said Rocky. "Big color photo in a wildlife magazine of our bear and her cubs." The idea grew and he waved his arms at an imaginary pinup. "Wouldn't that be great, her big furry face, just like she looked through the binoculars?"

Ned shook his head.

"Oh, come on, Ned. The photographer takes a picture of our bears, 'click!' then he's in Africa 'click!' with the lions, in Norway 'click!' with whatever they have in Norway. That's what they're like, wildlife photographers. Come *on*, Ned. Fifty bucks each and a big picture of our bears. I'll get him to send us one."

Ned was annoyed. How could Rocky take it so lightly? Ned hadn't received pocket money for months, but he wasn't tempted.

"They're our secret."

"Zounds, you're a worrywart, Edward," said Rocky. "I was the one who went looking for the bear in the first place, remember."

"She's *our* bear," said Ned.

"I'm meeting him at the crossroads," said Rocky. "I'm going to tell him." He turned to go.

"Okay," said Ned quietly, "I'll come with you."

Rocky stopped and scuffed in the leaves.

"Actually, don't come with me. He said he wanted me not to...well, to keep it private. He said he wanted a scoop, so...I shouldn't have told you. I mean I'll share the hundred bucks, but I don't think you should come with me."

Ned glared at him but said nothing.

"Meet you at Second Stream in an hour." He turned and ran off.

"At least ask him what *magazine*!" Ned yelled angrily.

As soon as Rocky was out of sight, Ned doubled back down another track. It was a long way and sometimes hard to follow because of the carpet of leaves, but it came out just before the crossroads. He ran till the blood pounded in his head.

Suddenly, through the bushes near the junction, Ned heard someone laugh. Someone with a deep voice, talking on a cell phone. Ned dropped behind a stone wall like a Minuteman and crept as close as he dared. He listened, hardly breathing.

"This kid knows the woods like the back of his hand. Saves Hank stumbling around with the damn camera. Yeah, meeting him now."

Then came a pause. A squirrel floated up into a tree.

"Why should we do the hoofing if the kid knows?"

Silence, except for the squirrel on a branch now, and the man's footsteps crunching in the leaves.

"Stop sweating. She's terrifying the neighborhood. They can't let their pets out. We're doin' 'em a good turn. Probably get hit by a car anyway...."

Ned strained to hear as the man walked away; then

with a laugh he turned back toward Ned. "…Dunkin' Donuts. Loves 'em. That's what the kid said. Some family he knew started feeding a bear. Yeah, Dunkin' Donuts! They've got a real sweet tooth. Been through everything the vet said a million times."

The vet? You don't need advice from a vet to take photographs, and you don't feed a bear.

Ned felt hot.

"Miss Bones take the lemur? You're on a roll, man. Stop hassling me."

Then the footsteps hurried away. Ned just caught a glimpse of a red-and-black-checked jacket disappearing between the trees.

Ned was totally alert.

I need Rocky. There are two of them at least. We confront them together. I'll catch him at the fork.

Ned flew back along the main track and waited at the fork, his stomach churning.

Come on, Rock, where are you? Taking forever! Oh damn! Must have missed him.

Ned raced back to Second Stream. At last Rocky jogged up the long path by the pond, wearing a grin that faded the minute he saw Ned's face. "What's wrong?"

The words tumbled out. "Heard one of them on a cell phone. Two men at least. Photographers don't talk to vets. They don't want to photograph the bears, they want to catch them!"

"Oh *no!*" cried Rocky, suddenly galvanized.

They ran like the wind. It was dangerous. Slippery oak leaves covered rocks in the path, and any second they could trip and hurtle to the ground, but with the bear at stake, they flew.

"I even told him about Dunkin' Donuts," Rocky gasped out between breaths.

They scrambled along the stone wall to the bear's secluded hideout, but it was deserted. No men. No bears. Just a nuthatch flitting down the tree trunk where the cubs had practiced climbing. They found the shelter the bear had hollowed in the hillside. Searching further, Rocky found where thick, low growing bushes and a tree had been snapped off and a strong vehicle had driven in.

Then Ned found the body.

She was still warm, but limp and lifeless. Blood oozed from the gunshot wounds and dried on her fur. Her large head lay as if she was asleep. Ned didn't make a sound. He dropped to his knees beside the bear, put his face in her fur and wept.

"They've taken the cubs!" Rocky was pitiful, his arms flailing hopelessly. "I'm sorry, I'm sorry," he cried over and over.

At that moment, Ned hated Rocky. He could have said, "I know how you feel," but he blamed Rocky, just as Kate had blamed him.

He held the bear's great floppy paw in his hands. He ran his fingers down her curved claws, so long and strong they could hold her weight as she climbed. The pads were like large rough mushrooms pushing through the fur. Beneath the black was the thick under-layer of fine fur that would've seen her through winter.

In the prime of her life. Why did they do this? Couldn't they see how beautiful she is? And powerful and intelligent. She protected her cubs, but we searched and searched and found her. What chance did she have? Because of us, she's dead.

"I could have *stopped* them if I hadn't waited for you." Ned was angry with himself as well as Rocky and the men.

Rocky wandered around the clearing in stunned misery. "I guess they had cages. I guess they tranquilized the cubs. They drove up the telephone cable road. They did it so fast."

"They stopped her with a couple of shots." Ned stroked her side and felt her ears.

"They might have found her without my help," said Rocky.

"Oh yeah?" snapped Ned. "Was she *easy* to find?"

"We can't bury her," said Rocky, distraught. "We'll just have to leave her."

They dragged branches from the broken bushes and laid them over the body, but it was impossible to cover her completely. They could always see something of the mound of black fur.

With heavy hearts, they trudged home.

"What will they do with the cubs?"

"Don't know," said Ned, "but on the Net I read that some Japanese men think bear pancreas is good for their sex life, and there are other uses for parts of a bear."

"They're just merchandise."

"Yeah."

"Will we tell the others?" said Rocky.

"That we caused her death?" Ned looked at him, incredulous.

Rocky never mentioned the money. First he threw it in the compost; then he dug it out, washed it and hid it in an envelope under his mattress.

18

The Hunk'o'junk

Martha couldn't put her finger on what was wrong, but Ned went quiet. The bear hunts stopped, and the friendship with Rocky seemed to have cooled, which was a shame because she liked Rocky. What had happened? She tried to get him talking, without success. She hung a bird feeder outside his bedroom window, although she knew it would take a week for the birds to find it, and she baked apple pie.

Then Janet found a car: a 1987 Chevy Cavalier sedan, black, with a little rust at the bottom of the doors.

Ned was disappointed. "Not much to look at."

"It was a good price, and Stanley the mechanic at West Concord Motors says it's reliable. Bit noisy," Janet added, "but when he's not so busy, he's going to fix it."

Martha appraised the car. "That's a fine-looking hunk'o'junk."

"Does it go?" Ned was sullen.

Janet patted the hood. "Course it goes, don't you, Hunk'o'junk!"

Then she went to climb into the wrong side of the car.

Janet turned the key.

Rrrurrr rrurr rrrurr bnang bang bang bang!

She tried again.

Rrrurr rrrurr rrurrrbnang bang bang gruuum brum brum!

The third time, the engine roared into life, bruuuum, bruuum, bruuuuum—an angry complaining roar, as if it had woken up in a bad mood.

"Sounds like a crack in the tube of the exhaust," said Ned.

"Steering's a fraction sloppy," said Janet. "About a half-inch slack before it takes up."

Their first expedition in the Hunk'o'junk was to buy new shoes for Ned. His toes were pushing through the front of his old Nikes. Martha briefed Ned as navigator, and they set out for a sale at a huge warehouse outlet.

Janet took her foot off the accelerator and coasted past police cars and police stations, hoping they wouldn't be noticed. She was racked with guilt because the Chevy was polluting and making such a noise, but she was determined to be independent, and Ned needed new shoes.

On the highway, everything passed them. When they did occasionally reach the speed limit, everything still passed them because nobody kept to the speed limit.

"Wrong way!" shrieked Janet. *"Ned! We're going the wrong way!"*

"It's *okay*! That sign's for the other lane of traffic."

"Is this Route 495? How can you *tell*? Why don't the signs tell you what you want to know? What does it mean, Cape Cod? What's this exit business? Ned, where *are we*?"

"Mam, there's a huge truck boring down on us."

"My God!"

"Put the pedal to the metal!"

"The speed limit's fifty-five. We're doing fifty-five."

"That truck isn't."

"I'm not going to speed. I'll attract attention."

"We'll be roadkill in a minute!"

"Everybody's doing sixty-five at least! We're attracting attention by going so *slow!*"

"We're on Route 495!"

"*Heaven be praised!* We're actually on Route 495."

Ned took a deep breath. "It said Route 495 *south.*"

"*What? South?* We want *north!* You mean we're going as fast as we can in the *wrong direction?* Ned, where *are* we?*"

They took an exit, found north and charged back along the six-lane turnpike for three-quarters of an hour, then bought two pairs of shoes because the second pair was fifty percent off, and drove home again.

Janet was triumphant, but exhausted. She went to bed early. Ned, however, sprang and dashed and stopped suddenly to test his new shoes. They had great traction and they were so soft. He hadn't realized how uncomfortable his feet had been. His spirits lifted a little.

The first time Janet drove to the supermarket, she locked her keys in the car, and who should help her but the "paperor-plastic" man.

"You locked your keys in the car, ma'am? That's wonderful, ma'am! You got a car!"

When he saw the Hunk'o'junk he said, "I don't think you need to bother locking this car, ma'am."

In the Hunk'o'junk they traveled far and wide. Gerry, from Bohager's Removals, tooted at them as he drove by in a huge van. Plant nurseries beside the highway advertised their chrysanthemums with signs saying "Hardy Mums." Ned and Janet smiled at each other. She was getting hardier.

Life continued. Ned and Rocky were still friends, although sometimes Ned sank into a strange, aloof mood. He remembered the bear at odd times. He hoped wild dogs had eaten her. He hated the thought of her just rotting away. And he wondered about the cubs. Would they be together? One thing was certain, they would be caged.

Ned and Rocky never went back to the secluded spot in the forest, and they kept their secret. They talked a lot about what Ned had overheard, about Miss Bones and the lemur. The words were so odd, Ned felt he might have misheard them completely, and it was frustrating because there was nothing they could do. The *Carlisle Mosquito* reported that the bear must have left the area because there had been no more sightings.

After several attempts, Ned finally told Kate. He finished by saying, "There's something about me that causes animals to be taken." He didn't expect any sympathy, and he didn't get it.

RM
Stop SLOSHing around in your Miseries
I gave you a REAL COwbOY CLUE
K   K   I   C   K   K   I
K K   I   C   K K   I
K K   I   C   K K   I
K   K   I   C   K   K   o
That's a kick up the pants!

His New York MANSION with tiger skinson the floor gym sauna
spaand guns swords HUNTting stuffed heads
YOu've got nEW shoes. RUN
Go to NY!

K
and t ell meALL theHallOWEEEEEN creepynesses.
aS for ROCky—i'm still talkign to YOU   Knuckhead

19

Fearful Things

Kuza

The sun sets early now. The trees are bare. Winter's closing in and First Stream is flowing. It's cold and dark. When I go to Rocky's through the woods, I run for fear of the ghosts of bears. Next Saturday night is Halloween and the stores are chocked with mountains of candy. Two houses down white plastic skeletons blow in the wind, from bare branches. People play at scaring.

BUT there are real creepynesses.

Near the big rotary (roundabout) on Route 2 there's an enormous PRISON. I pass it on the school bus twice a day. In the afternoon on the way home I see visitors going in, poor, lot of colored people.They are like from another world. All the well-off Concordians fly past on Rout 2. Last night I dreamt a prisoner burst into my room.

TOMBSTONESin the main street of Concord. Yes weakling, old cemeteries in the middle of towns not hidden behind hedges or walls. You know how you hold your breath when you pass a cemetry? You'd be fainting. Every day.
OOooooOoooooooo0000OOOooooooooowwwww!
RM

Abigail was scooping mush out of a bright orange pumpkin.

"It'll rot!" said Rocky. "You're carving it too soon."

"Do people eat those pumpkins?" asked Ned.

"Not me," said Rocky, "no pumpkin is an edible pumpkin."

"Hey, Rock, you know 'trick or treat'? What happens if they say 'trick'?" Ned asked.

"You egg their cars or splatter rotten tomatoes or spray Silly String, but usually you do nothing."

Dave strode in with fresh bread and the mail. "Hi, Ned. Do you have Halloween in Australia?"

"No."

"Very wise," said Dave. "I have a conspiracy theory. The dentists are in league with candy barons."

"What's a conspiracy theory?" Abigail was carving a mouth in the soft flesh of the pumpkin.

"The idea that 'they,' the people with power, manipulate everything so they get what they want."

"Say, for example," said Rocky, "if a trunkful of candy was stolen in A-Town, then another one stolen in B-Town, you'd think these two events were related. Could you have a conspiracy theory about that?"

"Yes," said Dave, gazing thoughtfully at Rocky's hands as he tried to fill an old fountain pen, "but it remains only a theory until it's proved. That'll never work; the bladder's perished."

Viv, Rocky's mother, bustled in. When Viv was home the house switched to top gear; the lights were brighter, time went faster and people paid attention. Then when she left it was back to happy old Dave time.

"You guys are too old to be trick or treating," said Viv. "It's for little kids."

"But Ned's never done it," said Rocky, "and do *you* want to slope around with the Munchkateers for hours in the dark while they trip over their costumes, count their candy and lose things?"

"Thanks for volunteering, boys," said Dave. "You've got the job."

"SCREECH! SCREECH! SCREECH!" screeched Abigail and did a high five with herself. "I'm going to video Halloween."

"You'll have to do it secretly," said Rocky casually. "People don't like a camera poked up their nostril. They get self-conscious, and you won't score much candy."

Abigail went off, deep in thought.

She returned sometime later and they could tell by the way she sang her loopy song she was very pleased with herself.

Ma Traveling Witch. Ma Halloween song.

Wa won't be short, wa won't be long.

Ma Traveling Witch. Ya diddle diddle diddle.

Na much at the end, na much in the middle.

Ma Traveling Witch..." and so on and so on.

The traveling witch wore an old backpack on her back, covered by a cape that gave her a strange hunched shape, and the whole outfit was dripping with roughly drawn spiders on strings. She had cut open a large, worn, brown soft-toy cat and stuffed the video camera inside it. She was such a mess, it took a while to notice anything in particular.

"I'm going to video like this." And she held the cat under her arm at waist level.

"*Ma Traveling Witch...*"

"We heard," said Rocky.

"You have to admit she's clever," said Ned when she'd gone.

"Never," said Rocky.

102

Ned hooked his jacket on the peg and charged into the kitchen, out of breath from his dash through the woods.

"I'm going to trick or treat with Rocky and the Munchkateers on Saturday. I need a costume," he panted.

"Not now, you don't," said Martha.

"Clean yourself up. Dinnertime," said Janet.

"Two mothers," Ned grumbled cheerfully as he stomped upstairs to the bathroom.

Each Saturday an avalanche of leaflets and catalogs fell out of the *Boston Globe*, but one in particular had caught Martha's eye. It was from a store called The Big Party and featured a spectacularly gruesome range of Halloween costumes. Martha combed through the pile of old newspapers till she found it, then left it on Ned's bed, where he would see it when he came home from school.

"We'll probably be late," said Janet, putting on her coat.

"Heaps late," said Ned, goggling his eyes and flapping his tongue at Martha.

It was dusk and drizzling with rain as the Hunk'o'junk roared out onto the highway toward The Big Party in North Chelmsford. The wipers wheezed and scratched at the windshield, adding to the din of the exhaust.

Ned was navigator, as usual. He took the job very seriously and had become skilled at giving Janet the information she needed at just the right time. He knew the highway number system now and how to negotiate the entrances and exits. Janet trusted him.

For Janet, driving was a challenge she seemed determined to meet. She hunched forward over the wheel, peering through the wipers, her face a study in grim determination. She drove even more carefully than usual as the reflections of headlights made moving ribbons of light on the wet roads.

"Seven dollars is your limit," said Janet.

Friday night before Halloween was a shopping frenzy at The Big Party. It seemed like a party was already in progress, with people squeezing past each other, trying on costumes and masks: Laughing Darth Vaders, sexy cat devils, three-year-old goblin twins, shrieking Frankensteins. Ned checked out the CDs of spooky sounds, glow-in-the-dark cleavers, black lights, plastic skeletons of all sizes, jumbo spider webbing, a wide range of fangs and a gruesome selection of severed limbs.

Ned tried on the range of masks and chose carefully— a half-melted face. It was good. It matched his skin color and he could still talk. He was scaring himself in the mirror when a bright voice behind him said, "G'day, Aussie!"

It was Rosangela from the motel, peering at him from under a green wig that reached to her knees.

"That looks very nice," she laughed. "How ya doin'?"

"Fine," said Ned, taking off the mask. "The lady came home and we're okay now. Great wig."

"You found a snake yet?" asked Rosangela.

"No."

"There was a guy on the next street who likes animals. Maybe he was a wildlife photographer, I think."

"Really?" Ned suddenly felt hot. "Is he still there?"

"He had a van but I haven't seen it around."

Ned's mind raced. He tried to sound casual. "Where was he? I'd like to talk to him if he's still about."

"You know the prison houses in Assabet Road? The last one."

"Cool. Thanks for that. I'd better go."

"Have a great Halloween, Aussie," said Rosangela.

"Thanks, you too."

Ned searched frantically for Janet, dodging hunchbacks and Frankensteins. He found her staring at a mutilated hand.

"I've got a mask," said Ned. "Let's go."

Janet gave him a look of surprise. She had expected to be there for at least another hour.

"Ned wants you," Abigail yelled down into the basement. "His light's flicking like a lighthouse in a storm." She had figured out their code long ago.

"Thanks." Rocky put on his coat and ran over to Martha's.

Rocky listened carefully to Ned's story, swiveling on the chair, fiddling with a broken cigarette lighter. "Gadzooks, I know those prison houses. They're going to be demolished."

"They're pretty scary."

"Gosh sakes! If the photographer's there," said Rocky, "I'd recognize him."

Then Ned had the brainwave. "We *trick or treat them* tomorrow night!"

Rocky's eyes narrowed to slits. He gave the thumbs-up sign in slow motion. "And the traveling witch…" He mimed Abigail operating the cat video.

"And we trick them, *hard*," said Ned, "with superglue!"

"Whoa boy, stay cool," said Rocky, "Don't wreck investigations. One step at a time."

"They'll pay," said Ned.

20

Halloween

If anyone had seen Ned crossing First Stream by the light of Martha's flashlight that night, they would have been terrified. His clothes were splashed with blood.

Rocky's place was in a frenzy. The Munchkateers, for some unknown reason, had called themselves the Wicked Witches of the North, South and West. Kari was Cleopatra, Jade a white rabbit and Abigail, the traveling witch, looked sensational with her dark skin. She dripped with extra spiders, her cat was now sprayed black, and as a last touch she asked Ned to drape her with fake web. "Not in front of my cat," she said. "My cat wants to see."

Rocky started doing an excited little broken-wing bird dance, his head jerking forward, raccoon fingers fluttering. Ned watched and laughed.

"They always laugh at his dance," said Abigail. "Funny, isn't it?"

"Please be polite and responsible," said Dave, looking Rocky square in the eye.

"Yes, sir!" Rocky saluted, and pulled on his ape-skull mask. They set off.

Flickering jack-o'-lanterns glowed with manic smiles from the front steps of all the houses. Plastic skeletons flapped in the night breeze. Neighborly porch lights illuminated bizarre little dramas enacted by the oddest characters. Spirits, witches and ghosts drifted from house to house, screaming and laughing. The night was abuzz with madness.

"First we'll do our side of the stream, then your side." Rocky caught Ned's eye.

"But we'll have to walk through the woods in our costumes!" said Abigail.

"What about the bear?" said Jade.

"The bear's on vacation," said Ned.

"Twice the candy!" said Rocky.

The witches agreed.

"Act the part," said Rocky. "Then instead of saying 'Take two! Only two!' they say 'Grab a handful.'"

Ned watched people's faces as they stared at him with gruesome fascination. The side of his skull appeared to be melting in pale cream candle-fat drips, leaving tendons and bones exposed. Encouraged by their reaction, he bent forward as if writhing in agony. It was hot and rubbery behind the mask, but the effect was worth it. The candy rolled in.

An hour later, after comparing loot with kids from Rocky's bus, they crossed First Stream. The Munchkateers were getting tired.

"One street to go," said Ned, nudging Rocky.

"Best for last," said Rocky.

"This is a long way," grumbled Jade. "The houses down here don't look very good for treats."

"This is near the prison," complained Kari, traipsing along behind. "I hate this place. I want to go home."

Ned and Rocky cajoled them on. "Just a little farther. These are *real* Halloween houses. Don't they look cool? Are you scared or something?"

The last house was forbidding. A window shutter hanging by a couple of hinges squeaked and bushes rustled in the overgrown garden. A Land Cruiser and a black pickup truck were parked beside the house. There was a light on in the front room behind a torn blind. No cheerful lantern flickered on the steps.

"Is this a joke or something?" said Abigail.

"This is real Halloween stuff for your cat," said Ned. "We brought you here specially."

"Spooky enough," agreed Abigail.

They assembled on the porch, with Cleopatra and the rabbit at the back. Ned's knock on the door echoed inside the house. Heavy footsteps walked toward them; then the door swung wide framing the silhouette of a tall man in working clothes and boots.

"The porch light's not on," he growled. "Clear out."

"Trick or treat," said Rocky.

"You heard what I said!"

Ned and Rocky peered past him into the house.

Suddenly the man hunched his body over, flung his arms high, and with his fingers pointing down like spikes he lunged at them: *"Aaargggh!"*

Abigail, Ned and Rocky stepped back, but Jade and Kari ran screaming down the steps.

"Get your delicate little candy-suckin' bodies out of here before I bite your heads off," the man laughed after them.

A second man came to the door. Silhouetted in a large shapeless jacket, he appeared to have no neck. He grabbed an ax from beside the door and brandished it. "I'll give you a trick you won't forget."

They fled with their bags of candy banging against their legs.

"Photographer?" panted Ned.

Rocky whipped off his mask. "No. Recognize the voice?"

"Maybe," said Ned, uncertain.

"Why did we go *there*?" Jade screeched at Rocky. "They were *awful*."

"Horrible!" said Kari.

"My cat liked that," said Abigail.

"We took you there because it was scary," said Rocky. "After all, it's Halloween."

"He was going to chop us up," said Abigail.

"Phooey! They were *joking*," said Rocky.

"Not funny!" said Kari.

"Did you see all the beer in the hall?" said Ned.

The Munchkateers hurried ahead. They soon cheered up, and by they time they arrived back at Rocky's, the haunted house was the feature of the night and the men were definitely aliens.

"Okay, Abigailforcewinds," said Rocky, "show us the cat video."

The cat video was dark, atmospheric and mostly blurred images of people's legs, bushes and bits of door. Nobody suspected the cat, and in one weird shot an old man's hand actually reached out and patted it. The funniest shots were of a dog that jumped for biscuits, bounding up into the frame, and the sudden flash of a crazed pumpkin face. The sound was great. You could hear the excitement in people's voices and the ridiculous things they said.

But the best part of the video was the haunted house. It had the feeling of real horror.

"That's the Hunter's leg."

"Here comes the werewolf bit!"

"Freeze it."

Abigail stopped the video on a graphic blurred image of the Hunter's hands.

"Wow, look at those fingers. Like someone put them on in the wrong order."

"They've been broken," said Dave, watching from the door.

"Here comes the Axman!" Their squeals of fear were chilling. Abigail was triumphant. She *loved* it.

She was rewinding the haunted house for the fourth time when Janet called, worried and cross.

"Got to go," said Ned, flying out the door. "See you tomorrow."

Late Sunday morning, Rocky burst into Ned's room like a jack-in-a-box exploding with candy. "Get out of bedward, Edward!" Candy rained everywhere.

"Oh man, you're as bad as Kate. Here, have a treat!" Ned leapt up and caught Rocky with his bagful. The floor was covered with a strange hail of sweets.

They sat on the floor and arranged them according to variety.

"This is fifty times more candy than I've ever got in show bags from the Melbourne Show," said Ned. "More than I have ever eaten in my whole life put together."

"Pile the Red Hots over here," said Rocky.

"Why do you think they're staying in that old house? Give me the Jolly Ranchers."

"They aren't office workers," said Rocky.

"No way," said Ned.

"They looked like hunters. Wow, see how many Starbursts we got!"

"They're sort of camping in that house. They had their jackets on inside."

"What are you doing this afternoon?"

"Same as you," said Rocky with a sly grin, the white wand of a Chupa Chup sticking out the corner of his mouth.

21

Two Men Drinking Beer

They walked toward the end of Assabet Road, keeping trees and bushes between them and the haunted house. The Land Cruiser and the black pickup were still parked out front.

"Gulp! Hazardous!" said Rocky, but Ned was already sprinting lightly toward the Land Cruiser.

"I feel like a cop in a TV stakeout," whispered Rocky, dropping down beside him. Staying close to the wall, they crept along the side of the house. At the corner they nearly leapt out of their skins when a voice from somewhere above said, "...tweetie bird feeders..."

They stole a glance around the corner. Two men sat smoking and drinking beer at the top of a flight of steps at the back door. The boys crawled round beneath them.

"...nerdy kids...fluffy dogs..."

The Hunter was in a talkative mood. Looking up between the boards, Ned and Rocky could see the thick soles of his boots, the seat of his jeans and a worn red-and-black L.L. Bean jacket. On the other side sat the Axman, silent.

The smell of tobacco wafted around. Afternoon sun shafted through the trees. A breeze rustled the branches, and a flickering shower of golden leaves drifted down.

"Look at that, isn't that beautiful? Last of the color. Makes you want to be sitting outside a tent somewhere, doesn't it? Anywhere but here," said the Hunter. A couple of squabbling squirrels chased across in front of them. Quick as a flash, he whipped an imaginary rifle to his shoulder. "*Ptew! Ptew! Ptew!* Squirrel pie!"

Ned and Rocky ducked instinctively.

The Hunter sighed. "I miss the mountains, I miss my dogs, I miss my horse, I miss my girl." He sighed again. Then he opened another can of Bud with his disjointed fingers and cheered up. "*Revenge with a Vengeance,* now *that* was a flick! Ann Blyth was leading lady. Frank did some of his best work in that movie. Seen it? 'Member that car comes in from the right-hand side, *pow!* hits the barrier, double flip, *pow! pow!* ramps it, crash *boom!*" They could see his arm waving as he acted out the movements in the air. "*Boom!* He hits his brother. Last job he ever did in Hollywood.

"That's Frank for you," the Hunter went on. "You know, despite the scandal, Frank was real proud of that film. He thinks he's the star in that film. Ask anybody what they remember about it, they tell you the chase. Not an actor in sight."

The Axman spoke for the first time, quietly. "Yeah, but they *think* the actor's driving."

"I know, I know."

"Hospital?"

"Concussion. Between you an' me Frank's got nothing left to concuss. Frank said Jay did himself in. Reckon Jay would suicide? You know the rumor about Jay and Maria...."

"Murder?"

They sat in silence for a time.

"That film was jinxed. They used the shot. They always do when a stuntman dies, but it soured the film."

He stubbed out a cigarette, and when he began talking again after lighting another, his mood seemed to have turned black.

"Frank's changed since the accident. I don't see eye to eye with him anymore. Just between you and me, right, I reckon he's lost the plot. The bear was like takin' candy off a baby, but I mean, a cheetah to Fitchburg for Christ's sake…"

Rocky flashed a look at Ned and grabbed his arm. If Ned had had a pin, he would have jabbed it up between the boards.

"…to Thenay or how you say it, and he's got some drug baron getting birds in Colombia, he's got an anchor man in Kingston on the seventeenth. He's building a drug scene; he'll get you anything you want as long as you pay.

"You know that devious Costa Rican, Fico, who's working for him? Mad as a rattlesnake. A hit man freelancing till things cool down back home. Some of the types he's dealing with are bloody nutters. I mean there's work and *work*." He took another long draught of beer. "I like to sleep at night." He wiped his mouth. "But you can't *tell* Frank anything, he knows the whole bloody lot. Guess what Fico calls him?"

"What?"

"Mr. Big."

The Axman snorted. "Hank still flying helicopters?"

"He'll fly anything that flies."

"Stunts at shows?"

The hiss of another can of Bud. "Adrenalin junkies, the lot of 'em. Well, Frank can risk his own life ten times a day, but I'm damned if he's going to risk mine. After this little bit of baby-sitting his brat in the bin, I'm out."

The Axman grunted.

"Frank always knows someone who owes him a favor. Well, he's calling in the favors now all right."

For a couple of minutes nothing was said.

"That man's got a mean streak. Always had this little chip on his shoulder but now it's a darn tree trunk. An' he's gotta have money. Money money money. 'Member when he gave Maria the ring? No, that was before your time. She wanted to go into fashion, but Frank bought her this ruby ring and stuck 'er on the end of the phone. Now she's calling him Boss and he's givin' her capital H, E, L!"

"Double L."

Then the conversation swung to the merits of certain brands of tire and the technicalities of ramping. Ned and Rocky crawled back around the corner and left the two voices sinking slowly into a drunken torpor.

The first stars were already shining in the darkening sky as they hurried home, and everything felt unreal. They were walking through the movie set of a thriller. They gabbled details at each other, desperate to remember it all.

"Frank!"

"Yeah, Frank."

"What was the film? *Revenge with a Vengeance*?"

"Yeah, Hank's the pilot."

"Cheetah? Cheetah somewhere?"

"Fitchburg! Soon. Thenay?"

"He's ripping animals out of *everywhere*!"

"What's ramping?"

"He's dealing drugs."

"'Like takin' candy off a baby,'" said Ned quietly.

"I know," said Rocky.

When the house was quiet that night, Ned emailed Kate and told her every single thing he could remember, every detail, because he knew Kate would come up with ideas.

Kate replied the following night.

HOLYCRIMINOLI!!!!!!!!!!!!!!!!!!!!!!!!

22

Revenge with a Vengeance

The video store closest to them didn't have *Revenge with a Vengeance*, but the one on Route 2 did.

"Wild car chase," said the pimply kid behind the counter as he snapped shut the case. "I think a guy got killed in it."

"Watch it at your place?" asked Ned.

"With the Munchkateers?"

So, when Janet and Martha set out on their walk, Ned and Rocky slotted in the video. It was dreary.

"Zounds, they could have used cardboard cutouts instead of those actors, and saved a lot of money," said Rocky.

"Yeah, cardboard would have done a better job," said Ned, fast-forwarding.

But the stunts were electrifying.

"Wow!"

"Cool! That must be him."

"This is it. This is the car chase."

"Holy *moly*! Look at *that*!"

They leaned forward, catching every detail as the car clipped one thing then another, hit the barrier, slewed sideways and took off into space. Then the car fell in slow motion, and the body hit the ground.

Ned felt his heart tighten in his chest. He saw his mother swinging in with the frying pan.

"I've seen this before!" he whispered.

"You okay?" said Rocky. "You've gone white!"

I'm locked in. Like landing wheels locked down. Like a padlock on a circle of chain. This was the beginning of it all. The reason why we're here. Somehow this is meant to be.

The film ended and the credits rolled up. There it was, first name on the list.

Stunts

Frank Laana   Hank Laana   Jay Laana

"Frank's our man," said Rocky.

Each night, after Martha climbed the stairs with her book and Janet folded back the Shaker quilt and went to bed, Ned searched the Web for information on Frank Laana. In the Stuntman's Slate Web site he found a list of films Laana had worked on and the people he had doubled for. He found his agent's e-mail address, an article from the *Los Angeles Times* and another from a stunt association newspaper.

Ned checked out stunt sites and read about high-speed reverse 180s, drifts in dirt, ramping, and flipping cars with a mortar. He scribbled it all in a notebook.

Dear Mr. Zilberman,
My name is Joseph Blake. I am fifteen. I am very interested in movies and I am a great fan of the stunts of Frank Laana. *Revenge with a Vengeance* is my favorite film because of the stunts.
As you are his agent I am hoping you can answer these questions about him.
Can you tell me where I can get in touch with him?
What other films has he been in?
Who has he doubled for?
Do you have a photo of him?
Has he worked with animals?
Yours sincerely,
Joseph

Ned thought twice about using Martha's e-mail address, but decided to take the chance and hit send.

~~

"Hello, stranger, how are you?" Martha was twisting stems of bittersweet into a wreath. "We got a rogue e-mail today."

"I'll check it out," said Ned.

"No, I dumped it," said Martha.

"I thought you didn't know how to do that," said Ned, feeling a knot of frustration. He went to his room and for an hour studied the instruction manual. When it was his time on the WebTV that night, he flexed his fingers and, with the concentration of a robber cracking a safe, steadily worked his way through a series of procedures. Finally, he retrieved the letter and sat back to read it.

Dear Joseph,
Sorry to tell you this, son, but sometimes it doesn't pay to get to know your idols. They don't look so good close up. I'll tell you the truth here: Frank Laana looks plain ugly. I don't work with Laana any more and wild horses won't get me near him again. He was a fine driver, but too full of himself and following a serious accident (when, as his agent, I supported his cause at great personal expense) he turned as bitter and twisted as a taipan in a knot.
He has a violent temper, a limp and no producer will touch him with a ten-foot pole.
Andrew Barton *(Demon Drag, Closer Call, Window to Hell)* is a fine stuntman and a nice guy. Want to know about him?
George D. Zilberman

Ned found a snippet in Miss Hollyrude's Gossip Column.

*Also at the party was wild stuntman Frank Laana, mak-
ing a splash with brother Jay, when a family feud came to
push and shove. Maybe lovely Laana, who suffered a
cracked rib, is not the handsome hair-loss-defying inde-
structible person he thinks he is.*

But the article that gave Ned the most information was
from a film trade site.

Background to the News
Risky Business

Not many lay people would have noticed the verdict.
It received scant space in the business sections of the
dailies, but a ripple went through the movie-making
world this week. During the filming of *Revenge with
a Vengeance*, stuntman Jay Laana was killed, and his
brother Frank badly injured, when a ramped car
stunt went horribly wrong.

In the aftermath of this tragic incident, well-
known stuntman Frank Laana and insurance company Rowland Mutual locked horns in a bitter battle.
Insurance for stuntfolk is high and the Laana brothers' company paid a premium as the result of an accident four years earlier.

The Laana company, Risky Business, compris-
ing the three brothers and Frank Laana's wife, Maria,
was once a flamboyant, successful operation based in
a large ranch in California. However, the court battle
added expensive legal bills to existing debts and the
company has now folded.

"All those years in Hollywood I bust my guts
for their movies," says an embittered Laana.

A representative of Black Ribbon Films went on the record. "It was proved beyond doubt that the deceased had not taken proper precautions, had failed to complete the insurance contract fully and, even if it had been completed, Frank Laana had also broken the conditions of the policy. Laana brought the accident on himself."

"Got something to tell you," said Ned, pulling his notebook from the pocket of his jacket. Ned and Rocky were sitting on the step where the two men had sat. The house was now empty and the street totally deserted.

Ned told Rocky everything he knew about Laana.

Rocky whistled through his teeth in admiration. "Jee-pers!" He slapped Ned on the arm. "You've got the whole doggone deal on this dude!"

Ned stared at his notes. "Now what do we do?"

"It'd make a good TV soap," said Rocky. "I could be me. You could be you."

"Yeah, that's what it sounds like. Like we made it up. Evidence? Nothin'."

"We could show them the bear."

"Yeah, I keep thinking about the bear. And the cubs."

"Wonder what animals they're ripping out now."

"I'm going to hunt *him*," said Ned.

"How?" said Rocky.

Ned shrugged.

They headed back. Just before Rocky disappeared into the woods toward First Stream, Ned stopped.

"Hey, Rocky!" he yelled. "Remotely! That's how I'll hunt him!"

23

Dancing at Starbucks

It was late the following Saturday morning when Ned, cruising along on Chris's bike, saw the Ford Mustang outside Starbucks, the coffee shop on the corner of Thoreau and Emerson. Ned carved a tight U-turn and swooped over. The Mustang had been extensively modified with reinforced door pillars and a custom-built dash with dials Ned had never seen before. Then he recognized the black pickup parked farther along.

"Starbucks! They're down at Starbucks!" yelled Ned, nearly falling down the basement stairs. Abigail was filming Rocky juggling clementines. He dropped two.

"*Quick!* Come on! Abigail, bring the camera!"

"What? What are we doing?"

"The Hunter and the Axman are at Starbucks. Do your dance, Rock! Abby, you video."

"What?"

"*Evidence!* Come *on!*"

They dashed past Dave like stampeding moose.

"What are those kids doing?" Dave asked himself. "Beats me. Something. Always something."

They made it to Starbucks in the time it takes to drink half a cup of coffee, and dropped their bikes to one side. The men were sitting at a window table to the left. Ned stayed out of their line of vision and flicked on the cassette player. Rocky stepped up and slapped his cap on the ground. Then, with his back to the window, he went straight into his broken-wing bird dance. There was a style about it. People stopped what they were doing and watched with half a smile. It was sudden, disjointed and crazy.

"Kids acting out a dare," laughed a woman.

Down on the corner, out in the street
Willy and the Poorboys are playing,
bring a nickel; tap your feet.

The music was loud and infectious. A roly-poly teenager in a group from Friendly's ice cream parlor opposite joined in; then his girlfriend and some little kids started clapping along. The people in the coffee shop laughed, and the Hunter and the Axman were laughing too.

Abigail was as bold as brass. With the camera jammed to her eye she could do anything. She set it on manual. Rocky was a blur in the center of the screen, but behind him the men were sharp and clear.

Ned didn't notice the red Ford Mustang cruising from the parking lot. It slowed to a crawl as the driver took a long look at the kids before gunning off down the street.

The track ended.

"Quick, let's go"—Ned grabbed the tape deck—"before they come out."

"Zounds! We're rich!" Rocky scooped up his hat.

"You should try Harvard Square," said the roly-poly boy to Rocky. "There's a heap of street acts there. You're funny, man, you'd make a mint."

They pedaled back to Rocky's.

"I got 'em," said Abigail, slipping the video into the machine, "all three of 'em."

"Three?"

"You watch."

It began with a close-up of Rocky's arm flailing out of focus, the music sounded like it was being played in a tin can, then Abigail established a good angle under Rocky's armpit and there were the men, crisp as a new dollar bill.

"Now, here comes Stoneface," said Abigail. "This shot's worth a Fribble at Friendly's."

Behind Rocky's arm, a blurred figure returned to the table, stopped and threw a suspicious glance at the camera just as the zoom ended and the focus cleared.

"Freeze it!" Ned was dumbfounded. The motionless face gave a cold stare straight into the lens. "The Cowboy!" he whispered.

"What's he talking about?" said Abigail.

"He's seen too many *X-Files*," said Rocky, laughing in amazement.

Am I blessed or cursed? Laana is the Cowboy. Of course I imagined it, with Dave's talk of conspiracy theories. But now it's true! It's like my number won the lottery from all those other numbers. But it's not a lottery. I know so much about this man. And once you know something, you can never un-know it.

It was almost too big to think about. The image of Frank Laana's frozen face sprang into his mind first thing when he woke in the morning.

Nobody heard a sound. None of Martha's neighbors.

Nobody. Yet it would have taken ten minutes at least, and the car was parked right in front of the house.

"Who would *do* such a thing?" said Martha, surveying the strange sight. The Hunk'o'junk was completely covered with Silly String. It looked as if it was draped in a monstrous macrame car cozy.

"That's a *lot* of Silly String," said Rocky. "Wow-ee, they've emptied three or four cans and it's not gunky any more. It's three hours old, easy."

"Is it an offense?"

"Kids getting rid of Silly String?"

Janet was upset. "Someone can't stand the noise. I'll ring Stanley again. This will be the third time he's promised to fix it." Janet didn't want to call the police because of the faulty exhaust.

Ned nudged Rocky. "Get in the car," he said quietly, indicating the front passenger's seat. And there, right in front of Rocky's face, glued to the windshield with Silly String, was a note.

BACK OFF OR WE'VE GOT
BETTER TRICKS THAN THIS

"Gulp!" said Rocky.

Ned slipped into the driver's seat.

"They know where I live and where I sit in this car."

"How did they find out?"

Ned shrugged. "They're hunters. But they don't know how much we know."

They picked off the Silly String and washed the car.

24

Kuza@work

Something set the camp dogs barking, which set Minga barking, barking, barking. Kate lay there with her eyes shut, refusing to wake up. She could hear crows picking at the rubbish in the gray light. She adjusted the louvers to catch any breeze, but the air was still. Too hot for anything. Then Minga began barking again. Darn dog.

Kate gave up trying to sleep. She tied a wet handkerchief round her neck, tiptoed to the study at the other end of the house and closed the door silently behind her. Taking a sketchbook from the back of the freezer, she settled cross-legged in front of the computer and logged on to the Net.

Scrawled across two pages of the sketchbook was a list:

Thenay
cheetah to Fitchburg
birds Colombia
anchorman Kingston 17
NYNY

Every time Kate looked at the list she felt angry. It was a shopping list of animals! How *dare* he swoop around the world snatching anything he wanted! If it was the *last* Oenpelli python, he wouldn't care!

She sat at the screen until sunrise, busily tapping and clicking, occasionally scribbling in the sketchbook. When she heard Ray's footsteps stumping to the toilet, she sent the e-mail, hid the book and slipped back to her room. In the gum tree outside, raucous squawking cockatoos were complaining about the new day.

Remote Man

France has two Thenays. ONe is in the middle in a bit called the Loire Valley. It's got castles. Now I'm thinking what is wild there for the Cowboy to catch? Not much deer boar ?maybe don't know But castles? people with castles have big mobs of money. So matybe something TO Thenay I'm thinkins, like a CLIENT in Thenay.

cheetah to Fitchburg   cheetah from??????? Africa
Fitchburg there's Fitchburg in MAss not THAT far away from you I don't think it's a rich place. Ask
birds in Colombia   too hard
anchorman in Kingston
There are 20 KIngstons in USA 2 on the sea
There are no aminals called anchors or birds or reptiles
Isthis man an anchor or does this man use an anchor ????
NYNY
This is areal solid CLUE
right near   YOU

I'M on the case.
Kuza

Ned found himself thinking about Kate's remark: "There are no reptiles called anchors."

The following weekend, Ned found an old tape deck at a yard sale. The kid had slipped in a Bob Marley tape to prove it worked. "Listen to that bass!"

"It's like being punched in the stomach by a noise," said Janet.

"Kingston," Ned said suddenly, back in Martha's kitchen.

"Capital of Jamaica," said Martha. "Next question."

"*Jamaica!* That's *it*! I'm at Rocky's…" His voice tailed off as his footfalls pounded away across the lawn.

"That wasn't much of a quiz," said Martha to herself.

"Not an anchor, a *nanka*!" gasped Ned out of breath, all smiles.

"What's a nanka?" said Rocky.

"Snake. Jamaican. Big. Huge. Yellow. Nocturnal. Rare. A nanka man in Kingston, capital of Jamaica. Get it?"

Rocky pulled a face.

"Well, that's what I think's happening," said Ned.

"So?" Rocky was trying to take apart an old Rubik's Cube with a knife blade. "You reckon someone will be nabbing a nanka in Kingston tomorrow?"

"Maybe."

He gave Ned a vacant look. "We're going to Grandma's for dinner."

"I'll tell Kate."

"What can she do?" Rocky was levering with more force.

"Who knows?"

With a sudden crack, the Rubik's Cube shattered into plastic shrapnel.

"Curses!" Rocky shook his head. "Totally unsatisfactory, Edward. We're fooling ourselves. It's all far away and out of reach. And if we do anything clever, they'll nail us."

Ned picked out Sneaky and set him on the comforter. "Yeah, Rock, I know, but it's a snake."

Despite Rocky's pessimism, when Ned heard Martha running a bath he tapped an e-mail to Kate and sent it anyway.

"Jamaica!" Kate liked the sound. "Jamaica? No, she wanted to." She chuckled at her own corny joke and turned on the modem. Kate had an original attitude to chat rooms. She imagined them like hotel room doors down a long purple corridor. When she wanted to know something, she raced down the passage, flung open the doors and shouted her questions into the rooms. This free-wheeling scatter-gun technique took her into schools, businesses, libraries, and a government department.

> **Kuza: Have YOU seena Jamaican nanka?**
> `MAcmacattaca: We had nanka pizza.`
> Toxic: Want some nanka hanky panky?
> **Kuza: I'm not interested in your pathetic jokes. Does anyone know about a nanka?**

Into another chat room. Then another and another. While she waited for the computer to organize itself, she picked at a bit of hard skin on her heel. She nearly ripped a hole in her foot when this reply popped up.

> Ja: There's a nanka in a bottle in the Kingston Museum, six feet long.

Babalooa: Six feet long!!!!!!!!!!!!!!!!!!!!!!!!!!!!!!!!!

Kuza: Ja have you SEEN it?

Ja: Yes. It's been there for years.

Kuza: Ja What IS a nanka?

Ja: A very large snake.

Kuza: Where is the Museum?

Toxic: Wanna see my nanka, Kuza?

Ja: East Street next to the library where I am now. Where are you?

Kuza: The Northern Territory of Australia

Ja: Why are you interested in the nanka?

Toxic: I'll show you my nanka if you show me yours Kuza.

Ja: I have to go.

Kuza: I'm DESPERATE to KNOW about the nanka! Can we talk more PLEASE!!!!!!!!

Ja: Half an hour earlier tomorrow.

Ja has left the chat room.

"Bloody Toxic! I could *murder* him."

Kate looked at the clock, took off half an hour and wrote down the time. She had no idea what day it was in Jamaica.

```
  \         /
   0       0
       U

      ___
```

25

Cleverton

Cleverton Lee was wedged in beside his grandmother, Hyacinth, on the crowded bus that crawled up Slipe Road. The sideman hung out the door and reached through the pack of bodies to take fares. Hyacinth handed him ten dollars Jamaican, which he folded lengthwise and wrapped around his fingers with a fan of worn notes.

Hyacinth smiled smugly to herself. "My Cleverton won't end up a sideman." She had insisted he be baptized Cleverton, and he *was* clever. He would be a professor or edit *The Gleaner* one day. He had a way with words all right, just like her, and now he could work a *computer*.

She remembered the first time he accompanied her to the library, carrying the heavy bag of mangoes for her friends. It was school holidays and Cleverton was glad to flop in a corner because the library was air conditioned.

Winifred, the librarian, saw him sitting alone under the hurricane warning sign and took pity on him. The library wasn't busy, so she showed him how to use the computer in the main reference room. He was a quick learner, and when she explained how to go on the Net, he was hooked.

The following day, the computer was reserved except for first thing in the morning. There he was when she opened the doors. Then she let him use the computer before the library was officially open, and it wasn't long before she was asking him to do things for her on the computer, and when it broke down she wanted him there to explain to the repairman what had happened.

This particular Wednesday, Cleverton's head was

spinning. For the first time, he had spoken in a chat room. He had talked to an Australian who was desperate to know about a nanka. He felt strangely delighted.

A young backpacker hailed the bus. Everyone looked down at his white face, pink from heat and exhaustion. The sideman shouted "All on! All on!" and everyone squeezed up as the bus lurched off toward Half Way Tree.

Chat's easy, thought Cleverton, like writing letters to his sister Clodine, who lived with relatives in Brixton, London.

Kuza: JA !!!!!!!!!! SO pleased to tap to you again

Ja: Hello Kuza

Remote Man: Hello Ja. I'm Kuza's cousin. Australian too but I'm staying near Boston in USA. And my friend Rocky is here too. We're all interested in the nanka.

Ja: Why do you want to know about the nanka?

Remote Man: We like reptiles. It might be my work one day. I keep lizards

Ja: Herpetology There are plenty of lizards in Jamaica. You don't have to keep them as pets, they're everywhere

Remote Man: Do you like reptiles?

Ja: They're okay. Most Jamaican's hate them. If my grandmother knew about the lizard behind my Bob Marley poster she'd scream the house down. Our snakes are harmless.

Kuza: We want to ASK you something and TELL you something. BUT firist we want to be sure that you are you?

Remote Man: Can you prove it somehow?

Ja: That's a googly.

The chat rolled up the screen.

"He's thinking," said Ned.

"He doesn't sound real," said Rocky. "What's a googly?"

"Way of bowling in cricket. I think it's a librarian. I mean, *herpetology*!"

"Probably a fifty-year-old crater-faced dumpling in Cleveland."

"Would it matter if it *was* a librarian?" said Ned.

Ja: Yes Check *The Gleaner*, Kingston's newspaper, February 4 about a spelling bee
Kuza: I will

Kuza has left the chat room.

Remote Man: Tell us about the spelling bee Ja
Ja: Saturday February 3 The finals at the Hilton Hotel started at two o'clock in the afternoon and I was in it.
Remote Man: What was the last word you had to spell?
Ja: fluorescent
Rocky: How do you spell obnoxious?
Ja: Just how you spelt it obnoxious
Remote Man: This is dopey.
Ja: Precisely
Remote Man: Did you get any words wrong?
Ja: No

Kuza has entered the chat room.

Kuza: *The Gleaner* said the spelling bee was on February 3 and the winner was ....your name <><> No miTAKES!!! !!! !!!!!!!!! beneficial psEUDonym circumstancelieutenant jostle fluorescent Ja you're a brain, like your name

Remote Man: What do you think Kuza?
Kuza: Good enuogh for me!!
Remote Man: Ja, where would someone look for a nanka in Kingston?
Ja: A live nanka? Maybe from a collector or in the wild they would need to go north. I could find out where.
Remote Man: Someone's coming. Bye.
Toxic: You betta believe it!
Kuza: Buzz off TOXIC!!!!!!!!!

Martha bustled in, annoyed. "Ned, get off that thing," she snapped. "Give me a chance to use the phone. I want to call Chris."

Rocky and Ned cooked popcorn in one of Martha's good saucepans and burnt the bottom. Ned scrubbed and scrubbed to get it clean, and by the time they reached First Stream Rocky had eaten most of the popcorn, and what remained was cold.

"Doggone it!" said Rocky. "It's hopeless, I'm not even on-line. You have to wait until late to get on the WebTV or we sneak on it, sharing the keyboard with that weird code. Kate's in another solar system, Ja won't have an e-mail address. The chat room is clogged with all that interrupting crud. *Tarnation*!" He kicked a rock and it fell into the water with a loud plop. "Chasing Laana's a fiction."

"Where exactly is California?"

"The other side of the continent."

Ned thought for a moment. He was trying to stay positive. "Just keep remembering the bear."

134

RM

NY NY ever hear THAT before?

It's 12mm dfrom Bostom on my map. Not FAR!!!!!!

K

PS

++++ A L A K A Z A R ++++++ (USA for U)

Alakazar ca-coct

Defloga hi! Idil inia?

Ka skyla MeMaryland!-

Mamimin, Ms Momont Nenv

New Hampshire New Jersey New Mexico New York

North C North D

Oh Ok! Or pari?

South C South D

Ten-texut   Vt-vawa

West V   Wiswyo

GetIT?

(the P O abBreviations roughtly)

Aren't I kind to you

Now you'll have

time for:

```
                                              _O_
                                             _|_|_
                                           _|_____|_
                                         _|_____|_
                                        |0 0 0 0 0 0|
                                        |0 0 0 0 0 0|
                                        |0 0 0 0 0 0|
                                        |0 0 0 0 0 0|
                                        |0 0 0 0 0 0|
                                        |0 0 0 0 0 0|
          _ _ _ _ _ _ _ _ _ _           |0 0 0 0 0 0|
         |  []  []  []  []  [] |        |0 0 0 0 0 0|
         |  []  []  []  []  [] |        |0 0 0 0 0 0|
         |  []  []  []  []  [] |        |0 0 0 0 0 0|
         |  []  []  []  []  [] |/|/|/|/ |0 0 0 0 0 0|
         |  []  []  []  []  [] | []  [] []|0 0 0 0 0 0|
         |  []  []  []  []  [] | []  [] []|0 0 0 0 0 0|
         |  []  []  []  []  [] | []  [] []|0 0 0 0 0 0|
         |  []  []  []  []  [] | []  [] []|0 0 0 0 0 0|
         |  []  []  []  []  [] | []  [] []|0 0 0 0 0 0|
         |  []  []  []  []  [] | []  [] []|0 0 0 0 0 0|
         |  []  []  []  []  [] | []  [] []|0 0 0 0 0 0|
```

26

NY & Nancy

"Why can't we go to New York?"

"Because we haven't got the money," exclaimed Janet, exasperated. "We're not fluffy-towel travelers. We could probably afford the train tickets and that's about it. Now change the subject, you're like a bear with two sore heads."

Ned shut up.

I was making all the decisions not so long ago, now I'm whining like a little kid. What can I do?

But Ned found an ally in Martha. "Now wait a minute," she chimed in. "I can understand what Ned wants. New York isn't at the end of the world. I'm going to call my good friend Nancy."

So Martha called Nancy and said she had Australian friends staying and the boy was passionate about seeing the dinosaurs at the Natural History Museum. How would she feel about some houseguests?

"She says, 'When are you coming to stay?'" relayed Martha.

Ned scribbled on a piece of paper, "AND ROCKY TOO?"

Martha smiled at this new information. "My young friend has a pal. Can you handle two boys aged thirteen?"

Martha beamed and nodded. "That's wonderful, Nance. You'll like 'em."

Then they went into a deep discussion about a mutual friend with anemia.

"All organized," said Martha. "You'll love her. She was my best friend at college, but our husbands never saw eye to eye. She lives alone on the West Side. You'll give her something to talk about for the next six months."

"Why don't you come too?" said Ned.

"Why would I want to visit New York? I've been there already," laughed Martha. "No, I like New York in the spring. Nancy and I go to the opera. We have a very nice time."

Ned signaled Rocky to meet at First Stream. Rocky could see by the way Ned bounded over the stepping stones that this was big deal.

"First the good news. We're going to the Big Apple. You too."

"Sweet!"

"Now the bad news. Mam's taking us and we're staying with an old lady friend of Martha's."

"Livable," Rocky nodded. "Right, we go to 40W72#2 and we knock on the door." He knocked in the air.

"Then?"

"We say, 'Would you like to order some Girl Scout cookies?'"

"Good one."

"Only problem is they always sell them in spring, but if you haven't got kids you won't know that."

"Do we have to carry bags of Girl Scout cookies?"

"No, you always get the orders first."

"Then we cook them?"

"Heck no! Some massive cookie factory cooks 'em. The peanut butter cookies are good. Thin mints! They're the ones adults go for, and you get a good quantity with them. Value for money. Stress that."

"Do you really sell Girl Scout cookies?"

"Yeah. For Abigail. The whole family does. She raised the most money in Acton last year. Mind you, Dad buys a year's worth and freezes 'em."

"What do we do after the Girl Scout cookie routine?"

"Whatever seems like a good idea."

That was the extent of their planning. Except for the clean shirt.

"Edward, take a clean shirt. This is very important. With a collar."

"Haven't got one."

"I'll bring one for you."

"NYNY! Can you believe it, Rock, we're off to the Big Apple. Good old Martha."

Ned used his time on the Net that night to research microwave ovens. He wanted to do something for Martha, and she definitely needed a microwave.

The train ride took five hours. It was six o'clock when they arrived at Pennsylvania Station on the island of Manhattan. Rush hour.

They swung their packs on their backs and stepped from the train into a raging torrent of people.

"Big Apple? Big Ants' Nest more like it," said Ned.

"Get over here, ant!" yelled Rocky, yanking him out of the path of a giant with a suitcase.

Getting from the Amtrak station to the subway was like swimming against a rip. First they were bumped and buffeted until they turned a corner, descended some stairs and were swept up in a surging crowd going their way. A saxophone wailed above the tramp of a million footsteps.

Janet wanted to climb on the train and go home.

"What kind of tickets do I buy?" she stressed as she inched forward in the line.

"To West 54th. We need the C train," said Rocky. "Blue. Not to the South Ferry. Over here."

Then the machine wouldn't read Janet's card. She tried it fast through the slot, then slow. She was causing a crush.

There's the wrinkle in the chin.

Ned vaulted back and swiped it.

The subway platform was poorly lit and narrow.

"*Look!* Subway rat!"

"Close to nature down here, Edward."

Ned studied the faces around him.

Masks. Every color of skin. Whoa, look at that dude, a black James Bond except more perfect. And that hair, braided and beaded. How does she sleep?

On a bench behind them lay a body draped in a filthy coat, a pair of blistered feet sticking out the end. A train pulled in with a piercing screech. The body didn't move.

Must be dead!

"Come on!" Rocky hooked him into the train. Ned found himself standing in front of a bear of a man with bloodshot eyes and a hat with worn fur earflaps. He was seated, and Ned's legs were jammed against his knees. Suddenly the man began ranting: "All five *bo-roughs*. Native American Indians are bearing down on the city *as I speak*. Total *an-ni-hil-ation*. Not *one* of God's creatures will survive. *Doom*. Ah say *Doom*!" He gave the word full, deep resonance.

Ned looked wildly around but nobody raised an

eyebrow. The man next to the mad preacher sat with his eyes closed, as if catching a little nap.

Oh boy! I may be Remote Man, but this guy's invisible!

The train lurched to a halt. Their stop. Ned pushed to get out, but he was caught by his pack.

"Let 'em off!" growled a woman's voice on the intercom.

People squeezed out of the crush onto the platform. The doors attempted to close, but Ned was jammed.

"Move into the middle of the car. The doors *are* closing!" said the disembodied voice, this time a tone higher and angry. "Makin' all local stops." Ned wrenched free.

Up out of the subway nightmare, they climbed to breathe the cold air and embrace the starry sky. By the light of a hairdresser's they stopped to get their bearings. Janet's hands were shaking as she unfolded the map. The city was battering her.

Two young toughs rolled toward them, ski caps pulled down. Janet laughed a little hysterically as one stepped close.

"Where ya wanna go?" boomed the deep voice.

"West 54th," squeaked Rocky.

"Four blocks up, take a left. Careful how you go now." They rolled on their way.

It's a virtual reality game, with multiple unknown players. Threats from any quarter, any time. Be constantly alert.

When Nancy opened her apartment door, wearing a happy-face apron, they were so relieved they nearly fell inside.

"Welcome! Welcome! We're having spaghetti," said Nancy. "I know you boys like spaghetti. Now, I want to hear all about you!" Her little old brown dog, Chugga, yapped at them, wagging her stump of a tail.

Nancy talked to herself when she wasn't talking to them or Chugga, and played classical music all the time, calling the singers and conductors by their first names. The table was set for four, and everything was homey and organized. Janet's bed was made up in the study and the boys were on mattresses behind the couch in the living room.

Janet and Nancy talked in the kitchen after dinner while the boys watched TV with Chugga, but before long they all went to bed. That was Friday night.

27

Saturday

"The Natural History Museum's in *The Guinness Book of Records*," said Nancy. "Largest museum in the world. Eat up, boys, wear comfy shoes, and it's a very doggy area, so watch your step."

The museum took up a whole city block. Together, they trundled through the dinosaurs, which *were* amazing, but their enthusiasm was a little forced because the dinosaurs weren't the main event.

"Mam, we look at things faster than you. How about we go off and meet you later?"

"Fine by me." She consulted the guide. "The Diner Saurus fast-service eatery at one o'clock?"

"Cool magool."

"Was that easy or what?" crowed Ned.

Rocky strutted like a millionaire. "Edward, my man, this is a classy neighborhood."

They ran past large apartment buildings with names like The Sander and The Wentworth, where doormen in uniforms dusted signs in marble foyers that read VISITORS MUST BE ANNOUNCED, and there were fancy little fences around the street trees with signs saying CURB YOUR DOG.

An incredibly long black stretch limo pulled up to the curb beside them, then the chauffeur came around and opened the door.

"Well, hooley dooley! Here's our car!" said Rocky.

But a sleek young couple appeared from nowhere and slipped inside.

"Bet it can't turn the corner."

It did. Ned laughed. It was all so far from a python on a rock in Wakwak.

The street numbers fell rapidly because the boys ran and the blocks were small.

"This is it!"

The number forty was beautifully lettered above the door in gold. It looked like a private house.

"It was grand, *once*," said Ned. "It's not Laana's, no way. Not his sort of place."

"Okay, Nedward, here we go," said Rocky, getting out the crumpled Girl Scout cookie order form and a pencil.

They climbed the steps to the front door. The catch had not closed properly. Inside was another set of impressive double doors in beveled glass. Ned saw his hand reflected in the highly polished brass plate as he reached out to push it. Locked. To the right of the door was an intercom grid. Rocky pressed #2.

Silence. They listened for what seemed like forever; then came a click.

"Yes?" said an old woman's voice.

"We're taking orders for Girl Scout cookies."

"That doesn't happen until February," crackled the voice.

"My sister's going for the *Guinness Book of Records* most number of Girl Scout cookies sold and we're taking orders already. What sort would you like?"

"I haven't said I want any," said the voice.

"Thin mints are value for money," said Ned.

"What's that accent?"

"Australian."

"He's from Australia."

"Is he now?"

"Yeah."

"Come up," said the voice. There was a click and a buzz.

Rocky pushed the door. "We're in!" he whispered.

They clattered up the marble stairs to find themselves on a landing before a new metal security grille. Behind it, in the center of the dark paneled door, was the most amazing bronze handle in the shape of a snake.

Ned saw it and nudged Rocky. Too late, they noticed the spy hole.

"Peanut butter cookies?" Rocky asked the spy hole.

"You're lying!" snapped the voice through the door. "Get out!"

"No, honestly! See, here's the order form." Rocky held it up. "My sister's so determined. You'd be her first customer today." Rocky talked and talked but there was no further response from behind the dark paneled door.

They clattered back down the stairs. Ned was bitterly disappointed, but Rocky seemed unaffected. "One old lady and a cool snake handle. Golly gee, she sure is locked up in there."

Once outside, Rocky went into detective mode. "Stay close to the wall so she can't see us," he said. "We're going to get in there, Edward." He strode purposefully around the block with Ned following.

"Sometimes there's a little lane or a fire escape.... Branches! There's a yard in the center of the block." Rocky talked to himself. "If we could just get up somehow...Yes! A fire escape! It's broken. See how it's slipped down? Geronimo, Edward. We're in!"

They waited an hour, but the light in the window stayed on. Besides, Ned couldn't see how they could reach the fire escape anyway. It was too high.

"Do you think if she hadn't seen the nudge she might have opened the door?" asked Ned.

"Who knows," said Rocky. "She's an oddball. Definitely something weird about that place."

When they came out of the bathroom on the ground floor of the Natural History Museum, there was Janet at the end of a long hall, deep in conversation with a white-coated museum official. As they walked toward her, the man excused himself and left.

"Right, I need food," she said brightly.

"Yeah, museum feet," said Rocky, flopping down at the cafe table.

Janet was jittery and excited. Ned was immediately suspicious when she offered them an ice cream after their homemade sandwiches.

"You know Chris in Tucson? Well, one of Chris's colleagues works here, and they want my opinion on a project that might involve Australia. Would you mind if I left you again this afternoon?"

"What do you think, Rock?" Ned looked worried.

"Yeah, we'll be okay, Mrs. Ned, in a pinch."

They wandered off at museum pace until they were out of her sight, then ran straight out the door back to 40W72#2. But the light was still on in the last room. "She's home, stubborn old duck." They ate donuts, sitting on a step waiting, but the light stayed on.

"We'll come back in half an hour."

To kill time, they followed four Norwegian backpackers to Strawberry Fields in Central Park. On an Italian mosaic set in the path, people had placed things in memory of John Lennon. There were three guitar picks, a Monopoly Get-out-of-Jail-Free card, Japanese coins and a long-stemmed red rose. Ned left a jelly snake from his Halloween stash. The Norwegian backpackers sang "Imagine," and Rocky joined in.

When they returned to 40W72#2, the blinds in the three front windows were drawn.

"The light's still on in the last room."

"What if she never goes out?"

"Tomorrow's the day," said Rocky. He looked at his watch. "We've just got time to check out FAO Schwarz."

"Who's he?" said Ned.

"Just the biggest toy store in the world."

They stopped running once—to watch a wild troupe of performers breakdancing in front of a large crowd, and Rocky neatly copied a couple of their steps. Then outside FAO Schwarz, Ned stopped with a jolt. A painted-up middle-aged crone with a basket sat in a ring of tourists. Ned stared at her shoulders. Clinging to them, like surreal epaulettes, were two chameleons in little harnesses, wearing clown hats and rainbow ruffs. The chameleons' eyes swiveled as the cameras flashed.

What is this? They're not rubber toys from FAO Schwarz. They're alive. They're real. From the bush, the jungle. What are they doing here?

He punched his fist into his hand.

"Freaky," said a little girl with stick-on tattoos on her cheeks.

"No, they're not freaks."

"I mean you," said the little girl, staring at him.

"They are freaks *here*," said Ned. "Everyone's a freak *here*."

Janet had Sunday planned down to the last second, so it took a lot of fast talking to revisit #2.

"We *really* want to see Strawberry Fields. It's John Lennon's memorial. I might never have the chance again, Mam."

"Honest injun, we'll be *fine*, Mrs. Ned. We'll be out with the joggers and back before breakfast."

"And we'll go to bed soon, so we won't be tired."

"Get your clean shirt ready," said Rocky as they brushed their teeth that night.

"What *is* this clean shirt business?"

"It's important, Edward. We need 'em. See, kids wear T-shirts all the time. People think boys in clean shirts with collars are nice boys."

28

40W72 #2 NYNY

Sunday morning, early, they danced down the stairs into the subway, their cards zipped through the slot, they could read the signs, they knew the right platform; in the virtual reality game they were scoring well.

"Edward, my man, all the ants are asleep."

They walked into a little supermarket just as it was opening. The girl flicked the switches and everything went on—lights, music, cash registers, signs, everything.

"Two donuts," said Rocky. "Do you have a bathroom?"

"There's a McDonald's round the corner."

The boys emerged from McDonald's looking as if they were off to church: washed, combed and wearing clean shirts. Ned wore his new best pair of shoes. They went straight to 40W72.

The blind was up and the curtains open in the last window. They buzzed on the buzzer with a story at the ready, but no answer came.

Ned had a feeling of rising excitement as they walked around the corner to the fire escape. He had no idea what was going to happen. Then Rocky spied a policeman on the other side of the street with a cup of coffee, watching them look at the fire escape.

"Tennis, anyone?" said Rocky, buoyant. When the traffic cleared, he bounded over to the cop. Ned watched, amazed, as Rocky talked to the officer who bent toward him slightly, listening and nodding, taking an occasional sip of coffee. Then they crossed back to Ned, chatting cheerfully.

"…did the same thing myself last year," said the cop. "You feel like such an idiot."

"This is my friend, Ned," said Rocky. "He's from Australia. He's visiting us."

"Hi, Ned. Having a good time?"

"Terrific, thanks."

The cheerful cop carefully rested his coffee on a step, then gave them a hoist up. "There you go. Your aunt's lucky to have you boys. I had to pay a locksmith sixty-five bucks."

Ned was still laughing as they clambered across the roofs. "What a con you are, Rock!"

"The power of the clean shirt, Edward."

It was difficult to know when they were above the right building. Ned steeled himself and peered down over the parapet to the street below.

"Yeah, this is forty."

Mindful of every sound, they climbed down the fire escape ladder to the landing. There was a window beside the back door.

"Hey, Rock. Security system. She's got the place wired like a bomb," hissed Ned. Rocky groaned quietly, then took a closer look.

"No, I don't think she has. She's got the stickers and the silver strips, but I think the old bird's doing it on the cheap! One way to find out. Get ready to bolt."

With his trusty old knife blade, Rocky slipped open the lock and quickly pushed up the window. Silence. They breathed again.

"This is seriously illegal." Rocky hesitated in front of the open window. "You game?"

"Jeepers, Rock, why are we *here*?"

They climbed into an old-fashioned laundry, very clean and orderly. No sound came from inside the apartment, and beyond the daylight from the laundry window, it was dark. They slipped across a hall and eased open the door opposite.

What they saw took their breath away. In the dim light they could make out a huge cavernous room of floor-to-ceiling glass display cases filled with the skeletons of animals. The hairs prickled on the back of Ned's neck.

That room opened into another, then another, like a museum, each rich wood-paneled room furnished only with display cases. The collection went on: birds, frogs, fish, mammals—thousands of perfect skeletons, some of the bones as fine as the finest needles. They were exquisite; each mounted, named and numbered. Slipping silently through the dark cold rooms, Ned was filled with admiration and fear. It was the work of a lifetime.

They sneaked back across the hall into daylight, into a smaller white kitchen that reeked of pungent cleaning smells. Spotless benches lined the walls, and above them was shelf after shelf holding white plastic storage boxes of all sizes.

"Not a kitchen," hissed Rocky.

"More like a laboratory...."

In the center of the room stood a stainless steel table.

"*Operating* table!" Rocky mouthed, eyes wide.

Slowly and silently, Ned took down the closest white box and lifted the lid. Inside was a bird, a macaw, that seemed to be moving slightly. Ned realized with horror it was crawling with larvae. The next box contained a rat-like animal, this skeleton also being cleaned by beetle larvae.

When the phone rang, it nearly sent them through the

ceiling with fright. An answering machine clicked on and a muffled voice left a message. Then, their ears straining for the slightest sound, they heard the unmistakable chink of a cup replaced on a saucer.

Ned's arm brushed a large pair of scissors on the stainless steel bench. They didn't fall, but they made a clear metallic scraping noise. Instead of sprinting to the laundry via the light hallway, they dashed back through the dark museum rooms. But whoever was there moved to cut off their escape.

They crouched in a corner and with terrified fascination watched the shadow on the floor moving slowly into the room. It was a gaunt figure with wild spikes on its head, carrying some weapon. Then, through the door, came a terrified old lady in a dressing gown, as frightened as they were.

"Huh!" Rocky exhaled as if he'd just got the joke.

"How *dare* you! How *dare* you!" she shrilled at them.

In her trembling right hand she held a large knife at waist height, as if to cut a slice of bread rather than inflict mortal stab wounds.

It's a B-grade nursery-rhyme mad-scientist movie… "she cut off their tails with a carving knife, did you ever see such a sight in your life"…She's a human stick insect, wasting away to a skeleton herself.

Her hands were almost see-through, with fine straight fingers. Papery skin stretched over her long bony nose, but her steely gray eyes flashed with life, and her white hair wisped up like storms on a dry-ice planet.

"What do you want, you presumptuous, impudent boys?" She made no mention of calling the police.

The knife clattered on a glass case as she dropped it. "Oh my, I need to sit down."

"God!" thought Ned. "What if she has a heart attack?" He dashed in search of something for her to sit on.

"We're not here to rob you," said Rocky.

Ned returned with a stool and she perched on it like an old heron.

"We want to know where you get them from." Ned indicated the skeletons.

She closed her eyes, considering her answer. "I don't ask questions, and you'd be wise to do the same."

"Do you order them?"

"No."

"From…?"

"I am not hurting anybody. I am not hurting any animals. Everything arrives in a state of rigor mortis."

"Oh, come on, they're alive before *that*!" said Rocky.

"Frank Laana, Miss Bones?" said Ned.

The tough old bird said nothing, but she was as taut as a wire.

"I'm trying to save what I can. My collection will show coming generations what richness we had." Her anger had died, and in its place was a tiredness.

"But some of these are endangered species," said Ned.

"Oh, some of them are already extinct. You don't believe they're going to survive, do you?" The wispy white hair waved as she shook her head. "They'll all be gone. You'll tell your grandchildren that you were alive when there were pandas and tigers on the earth. You'll tell them you ate fish from the ocean."

"But you're *helping* to make them extinct."

She shifted on the stool.

"I've lived a long time," she said in a weary voice.

"Human nature won't change. A leopard can't change its spots. Mankind is greedy." She closed her eyes again and sighed. "And nobody cares."

"No!" said Ned. "There *are* people who care. That's why we're *here*." He thought of the bear, and Kate's fury at the missing python, and Janet's fight to save the forests. "*Lots* of people care!"

"Rubbish," she snorted. "Children these days can't even name three birds."

"Do you have reptiles?" asked Ned.

"I do." They followed her into a fourth room. "They happen to be a particular interest of mine."

"Well, I don't know much about birds," said Ned, moving to a case of reptiles, "but I could tell you about these. That's a northern leaf-tailed gecko, that's a copper-tailed skink, that's a bearded dragon, that's a blue-tongue, you find them everywhere, that's a shingleback, they like yellow flowers, you find a lot of them squashed on the road." Ned saw skeleton after skeleton of the snakes and lizards he knew so well. He was sickened by the idea that this might, one day, be all that was left of them. Ned felt a sudden rush of longing for his lizards and the bush.

"Australian, aren't you, boy?"

"Ned, my name's Ned," he almost shouted at her.

"Wonderful wildlife. Thirty percent of your beautiful birds will be extinct by 2050. You ask your experts. *Experts!*" She spat the word again with scorn. "Experts have known what's been happening for years. The experts in museums are fools. Their collections are crumbling, the work is shoddy. I guess the public doesn't want reality. They want flashy things on screens. Computers and space—they're the new frontiers." She took a deep wavering breath. "We've dealt with this world."

She hadn't finished.

"They ask the big corporations for money. 'Sure. Here's a hundred thousand dollars.' 'Thank you, your sins are absolved.' It's easy feel-good money. They don't really care, they just push on."

"You think like my mother," Ned groaned. "She says that too. She's been researching a disease in trees for as long as I've been alive."

"Don't buy things from Laana," said Rocky. "He's evil. Besides, he'll rip you off."

"He says most come from breeders."

"You believe *him*?"

"Do you find registration chips implanted in them?"

"Please give us his phone number?"

"I haven't got it. I've never met him."

"He's greedy."

"He has excellent sources in Southeast Asia."

"But wouldn't it be better if all these were still alive?" said Rocky.

"Oh, get out, both of you," she said in a resigned voice.

She led them to the front door in silence and unlocked all the locks. She opened the heavy door, and there was the snake handle. Ned glanced back into the apartment and started with surprise. There, in pride of place above the hall table, was the X-ray snake painting. He had totally forgotten it.

"That Aboriginal picture was for sale in Wakwak for two hundred dollars," said Ned. "What did you pay Laana?"

"That's a very rude question!" she snapped, but her steely eyes were blinking with shock.

A smartly dressed young man with a frisky terrier on a leash was entering the lobby as they came down the stairs. He was consumed with curiosity.

"You visiting the old lady in number two?"

"Collecting for charity," said Rocky.

The man pulled a comic face and said with theatrical emphasis, "That would *have* to be a first!"

"Why?"

"Well, I've never even seen her, but I know she's tight with money. My friend who lives here"—he waved at the door of the ground-floor apartment—"wants to fix up the building but she'll only pay for the most basic repairs."

"Does she live alone?"

"I believe so, yes. Apparently she was a top surgeon back in the days when women didn't have such positions. They say she made a fatal mistake and lost her nerve. What charity, if you don't mind me asking?"

"Save the Animals," said Rocky.

The terrier was pulling at the leash impatiently. "Well, I hope she made your visit worthwhile," said the man.

"She did," said Ned.

Ned and Rocky were the first up the Statue of Liberty that morning. When they strolled off the gangplank from the Ellis Island ferry, they walked straight into another reptile event. A cluster of excited tourists were buzzing like flies around a black man stripped bare to the waist with a python slowly sliding around his muscular torso.

"How much?" asked a Dutchman, waving his camera.

"Five dollars if *I* hold it, ten dollars if *you* hold it."

A policeman strode around the corner. As if expecting this turn of events, the showman whipped the heavy coiling python into a bag, quickly shrugged on a jacket and walked briskly away—just a man with a bag. The crowd watched with delight; another twist to the show.

"Albino Burmese python," said Ned.

It was sunset when the train slid through Queens, rocked over Hell Gate Bridge, and headed north to the Bronx. They took a long last look at the island of Manhattan, the famous jagged skyline glittering in the soft pink light. Janet, on the other side of the aisle, was reading a little and dozing. She was tired but quite cheerful.

They slipped through cities and towns. The train was a good place for thinking.

"How was that python?" said Ned.

"Don't think he'd like the vibrations of the subway. Snakes don't seem to mind cars. Hope he took a taxi."

"You know how snakes sort of smell-taste with their Jacobson's organ? What would they make of the screeching heat and stink of the subway?"

"One sort of a jungle to another," said Rocky. "How was that old painted-up doll with the chameleons!"

"Chameleons in hats and ruffs? What is it with humans and wild animals?" said Ned. "Is it right to keep them like that?"

"But how can we know about them, otherwise?" said Rocky. "You've got your lizards. I've got my cornsnakes."

"They're happy, and besides, they're not endangered. That old witch and the python man, they're making a living out of them because they're freaky. In a city you only see dogs and cats and pigeons."

"People want to *possess* wild animals."

"Well, they usually die," said Ned.

"Everything dies in the end," said Rocky blithely.

"Is that what it's going to be like for wildlife? Little bits will remain on show as freaks?"

Then they sat quietly, rocking along in their own thoughts until they fell asleep around Mystic, Connecticut.

Kuza

We went there! And we got INSIDE!! Ask Rocky how!!!!

It's a private museum of skeletons created by a freaky old bird (about 80), as pale as if she's never seen the sun.

She's Miss Bones, no doubt about it!

She buys dead animals, birds, reptiles, snakes, all creatures, everything, prohibited imports, stuff from Asia, Africa, Australia everywhere She's fooling herself. She wants to believe Laana gets them mostly from breeders!!!!!!!!!!!!!!! She uses beetle larvae to clean the skeletons. Thousands of skeletons, a lifetime job She's doing it because she thinks the planet is stuffed.

Nothing alive in there except her, and she wasn't very alive. She dies, grubs eat her, collection complete!

She looked at us as if we were a new species! Couldn't get anything on Laana

What's hanging on her hall wall?

YOu guessed it. The red X-ray snake! She has a soft spot for snakes,

RM

RM

His phone no???
His email address????
Hiss address?????
Hismob ile??
His Fasx???
Thanks for NOTHIGN M]iss BOnes!!!!

K

29

The Jacket

Janet stepped shyly into the kitchen. She was wearing a skirt for the first time in ages. "I've been asked to speak at a conference."

Ned and Rocky looked up in unison from their game of crazy eights.

"The botanist at the Museum of Natural History told his mate in research…well, anyway, it's at Harvard."

"Wow! Great!" Ned studied her. This was big deal.

"How…" she faltered, "…how do I look?"

"Fine," said Ned.

Martha surveyed her, chewing thoughtfully.

"Martha?" Janet's shoulders drooped. "Well, there goes my confidence. I feel shabby."

Martha took a sip of coffee, tucked back a wisp of hair and rose to the challenge.

"You need to look *good*."

"No, no, I can't afford anything new," protested Janet. "Sorry I asked."

Martha sat up straight. "We're going to Filene's Basement," she announced. "Got my niece's wedding dress there, reduced from twelve hundred dollars. Guess how much?"

"Five bucks?" said Rocky.

"Give me a break! Fifty."

"What is it, a TV game show?" asked Ned.

"No," Martha laughed, "more like a treasure hunt in a football pileup. I need you boys."

They groaned.

Like all Martha's projects, it began with a flurry of phone calls to friends, to gather the facts. She pored over the ads in *The Boston Globe*, and next morning she caught the train downtown and was away for the whole day.

The following Friday evening, Martha briefed them. "The prices drop tomorrow. We're catching a train to Boston at seven-thirty. Timing's vital."

"Seven-*thirty*!"

"Shush!" said Martha. "Janet, wear those shoes and that skirt and be ready to try things on right where you stand."

"I don't think I can...."

"Ned, you're the tosser. Rocky, you're the catcher. Now, when Ned or I toss something over, you hang on like George Washington at Valley Forge; Rocky, you hear me? Don't let *anyone* take it from you."

Janet looked more doubtful every second, and Ned and Rocky hated the idea, but Martha was like a football coach at the Super Bowl. She sketched a map with the subway exit, the door of Filene's Basement, racks, pillars and counters, and drew an X where each of them was to stand.

Then Martha took the phone call she'd been expecting.

"Wonderful!" was all she said.

She was jubilant. "We're looking for a lime green shirt with a big purple zipper up the front."

"She'll look *lousy* in that," said Ned.

"There's a jacket underneath."

They were second row from Filene's Basement when the doors opened and the crowd surged forward. Hundreds of shoppers scrambled to be first to grab the big-name labels with the prices marked down. On a rack to the right, a stripe of lime green was clearly visible.

"Positions!" shouted Martha.

It was like swimming through a maelstrom of bodies and clothes. "Blass over here! A St. Laurent! Get the Fendi."

Ned reached the green shirt just as a teenager pulled it from the hanger. She wanted the shirt, he grabbed at the jacket. A blonde woman had the sleeve, but Ned jerked it from her. He gave a piercing whistle and tossed it to Rocky, who jumped for it. Three other arms shot out, but Rocky seized it. "Mine!" he shouted triumphantly, and held it close to his chest.

Janet tried on four jackets, but the first was perfect, and she bought it.

They battled through the tide of incoming shoppers to Downtown Crossing station, caught the subway to Alewife and were home by 10:30.

Janet was in love with her jacket. "Thank you, everyone. Oh, it feels so nice. Feel this, Martha, just feel it."

"What about her glasses?" asked Ned. "And she needs more hair."

When Janet came downstairs on the evening of the conference, she was nervous.

"Now that looks *smart*!" said Martha. "Mr. Gaultier would be pleased."

Poor Janet was excited one minute and terrified the next. Ned wasn't worried about her speech—she could talk about trees underwater—but this was the first time she'd driven alone at night, without a navigator.

"Bye, Neddie, wish me luck."

"Luck, Mam. And don't ask everyone to feel your jacket."

"Fancy a game of cards?" asked Martha.

"Yeah." Ned sat back. "I feel like the ground crew after blastoff."

They played at the dining table.

"This is major for her," said Ned.

"How do you think she's doing?" said Martha.

"Good."

"I do too," said Martha, looking out the window. A flurry of leaves swirled down. "I just hope…well…the end of fall can be kinda sad. All the creatures seem to leave us; they migrate south or go to ground. It can be kinda sad." She sipped her coffee slowly. "Lot of my friends don't like it."

Ned couldn't sleep. It seemed as though he listened for hours. Finally, he heard the far-off, unmistakable roar of the Hunk'o'junk. She was going slow, trying to drive quietly. He was out of bed in a shot.

"How was it?"

"Ned! You still awake? It was good. Go to sleep! You have to catch the bus in five hours."

She was standing in the hall with a huge bunch of flowers—tired, but smiling up at him. She looked a little like she used to look before she crashed.

The phone shrilled through the house, waking them all with a start. It was Rocky. "Janet's in the paper!"

There she was, mid-speech, impassioned, hands gesturing, eyes blazing.

"Wow!" said Ned.

Martha peered through her glasses at the photo with great satisfaction.

"What happened?" asked Ned.

"Well, they got their facts wrong." Janet pursed her lips. "They said I was sent here to do research."

"That sounds good," said Martha.

"But it's not *true*. Every nickel we spend is my hard-earned pay."

"Don't I know that!" said Ned. "Trust you to..."

"Shhh," said Martha.

"Honestly, I was shaking like a leaf. It annoyed me, but I kept smiling. Then, five minutes into my talk, a woman sitting at the front who didn't like what I was saying implied that I wasn't to be taken seriously. Well, I'm afraid the notes went out the window and..."

"You hit them with the frying pan!"

She nodded.

Martha folded the newspaper back and read it out loud.

DR. SPINNER SPOKE with great authority on the effects of dieback in eucalyptus trees, and of her horror at knowing native forests were being lost forever.

"Lines must be drawn. Hands off the wild places. Don't doze a road to every waterfall. Let those who want to, and who can, walk to them. Value the diversity, wonder and beauty. We delude ourselves if we think we can re-establish what was, so let's protect what we have, and don't let business touch these places. Business is like a cancer that takes hold and grows.

"Precious resources are being squandered, for what? We are robbing ourselves. The forests, the rivers, the seas, and the creatures that inhabit them, these are the treasures. Watch, listen, learn, but let the wild things be, in the wild places."

Sitting on the school bus next day, Ned thought about what she had said as he watched a formation of geese fly overhead. The bird at the apex dropped back and another took the lead.

Maybe we had to get that jacket. She wouldn't say those things in ordinary life. It was as if she was talking straight to me.

In the pressure and heat of the moment, Janet had found the exact words Ned needed to hear.

30

The Kelp Room

Kuza: There's a F*R**fWIT FfL*****ING F**Z**TFACe TOXICwho snoops me out and I can;'t say a thing in chat rooms or anYwhere everytime I open my MuTH there's bloody TOXIC that F*YT*KINg viper (sorry nEd I know theyre lovely) but I harpte his FL*S*King guts. He's looking for meEVerywgere!! He's giving me the totaly crfeeps Wat do i DO?

Rocky: Feeling better?

Kuza: im telling you ROckhe'll BE HERE &all we need is bloody TOXIC!!!

Remote Man: I know how you feel. Some freak wanted me to help him blow up the world

Kuza: well *****%#@*** sUGGEST SOMEthing somebudy quck!!!!!!!!!!!!!!!!!!!!!!! Ned your're tje wize guy. DO SAOMTHING! I'm loggign off. or he'll be here

Remote Man: Email you in ten minutes.

"What's happening?" said Rocky.

"She's being stalked. She can't shake this creep." Ned's mind raced. "Just let me think, okay?"

Ned was back on the Net, clicking around, opening up search engines—"Yahoo! no. Dogpile? No. Steam? Gopher?"—scanning list after list. "Where was it? This thing's so slow. I'll know it when I see it. Here we go! Got it!"

Rocky watched, mystified, as the home page of the Macroalgae Harvesters' Association prickled onto the screen.

"Seaweed?" said Rocky.

"Come on, come on!" coaxed Ned. Up came the list of contents. "Round Rock? Round Rock?"

"You talking about me?"

"There it is. Password? *Neptune*. Second password. What did I use?"

They stared at the empty screen, then a heading shuffled into focus. Written in flowing golden-brown straps of seaweed were the words WELCOME TO THE KELP ROOM and then, like an object flung up on the shore by a rogue wave, a single message appeared.

> **Remote Man: Kelp! Kelp! I'm drowning!**

"You *bewdy*!" Ned leapt up, spun round, sat down and typed in a new message.

> **Remote Man: I'll save you.**

"Rocky, my man"—he typed a pretend keyboard on Rocky's arm—"we have our very own cozy little underwater private chat room! With very good locks on the door."

Rocky was mystified. "Why are you chatting to yourself?"

"Tell you in a sec."

Ned closed the layers of screen behind him, jotting them down on a numbered list as he went, concentrating like a pilot checking for landing. Then he e-mailed the list to Kate. Then he opened his way back through the layers to the Kelp Room and tapped in:

> **Remote Man: G'day Kuzaly!**

Ned sat back with his arms crossed.

"What's happ—"

"Shhhh, just wait!"

They stared at the TV screen.

Welcome to the Kelp Room

Rocky: Howdy GIRLO!

Remote Man: You made it!

Kuza: FABBY-YOU-LUS! Fresh AIR! Nomore ToOXIC dumpointg tosixicness onme!!!! This is so so sogood Oh Peeples wondr OUSE PEACE He was even HACKling into my DEREAMS.!! HOww did you find it?

Remote Man: Checking out seaweed months ago in Melbourne.

Kuza: YOu chekc out seeeweed regularly? Why dosen't ainyone use ti?

Remote Man: I think the Macroalgae mob got some kid to design the site—a gamer like me, maybe the boss's son—back when everyone was playing Dark Knights. It's definitely based on Dark Knights. Great game. But I don't think he told the kelp growers how to use it.

Kuza: too busy GROwign klep?

Remote Man: I think they forgot the second password.

Kuza: Hey, Rock, I thought you didn't have email.

Rocky: I don't. Ned's figured out this code. We both use the same keyboard. We're good children. We SHARE.

Kuza: I'm telling Ja about the kelp room.

Remote Man: Tell an atom of this on a chat room & it's Hello Toxic time. Get a fax number.

Kuza: You thnik I want TOXIC!!! this is AIR for me I can BREATHE agian

Cleverton Lee collected two faxes: one from the Australian High Commission and one from the Bob Marley museum in Hope Road. He was the only boy in Jamaica to receive two faxes that day, and he was definitely the only kid in the whole Caribbean to spend the afternoon deciphering a code.

Kate was first to log on. Ever since she'd met Ned, her life was full of international wondering: wondering what Laana was ripping off now, wondering what time it was in Massachusetts, wondering if Ja got the faxes, wondering what Rocky looked like.

Kuza: [X]OOOooooooooooooooooooooooooooOOO [X]
 O o O o OO oo   WELCOME JA !!   o O OO o OO
Jamaicna flag - [X] ooooooooooooooooooooooo [X]
    O o OO   O o O o O   O   o O OO O o OO
Remote Man: Hi Kuza! LOve the decorations.
Kuza: Like the balloons? Searched the Top End for them. Help yourself to refreshements over by the swimming pool.
Remote Man: BANG!
Kuza: Yeah I nkow I blew some of them up too high
Rocky: YOu don't often see three foot swquare balloons with gold fish in them.
Kuza: I trained them too JUMP FISHIES!!
Remote Man: Do you really think he'll make it?
Kuza: Don't say anymore oryou'll chase my decorations off the screen.

They sat watching the screens, Kate in the heat of Wakwak picking at her toenails, and Ned and Rocky side by side on Martha's couch in Concord, chewing their chewing gum faster than usual.

Ned checked the time. "If he doesn't come soon…"

Ja: Good afternoon Ladies and Gentlemen. It is a beautiful day for cricket here at Sabina Park

Remote Man: Greetings Ja greetings !

Kuza: SO glad to read you.

Ja: That code! (or as you would say – tHat cdoe!!!!!!!!!!!!) This is excellent. We can talk freely. (Winifred at the library desk asks why I am laughing) Toxic is missing you Kuza but as my gramumma Hyacinth says—"Cackroach av no bisness a fowl dance"

Kuza: Isn't it cooL!

Ja: I have news. Winifred told me a man came to the library yesterday asking about reptiles. She said I was researching the nanka and he wants to meet me. He's a wildlife photographer.

Remote Man: There's our nanka man!

Rocky: You MUST MEET HIM

Ja: I can't. I'm going to stay with my uncle near Port Antonio.

Kuza: groan %$@%&#*

Ja: Who is he?

Kuza: double groan #$%@$#%$#@!!!!!

Remote Man: Okay Ja, here's the story. There's an ex-stuntman in Los Angeles who is ripping wild animals out all round the world. His name's Frank Laana and this "photographer" is probably working for him.

Kuza: smuggling & selling

Ja: An international poacher?

Kuza: EXATCLY

Remote Man: We can't get near him. We had five clues.

Ja: Keeps hitting you for six over square leg?

Remote Man: yep

Rocky: What do we do?

Kuza: Make a time to meet Gotta go.

31

Turkey Time

Martha cleaned everything for Thanksgiving. The windows gleamed, the floors shone, and the big fridge was emptied, ready for all the food. Following the success of the jacket it was her next project. Chris wasn't coming home, so she had invited the Rockys.

When Ned went downstairs the morning before Thanksgiving, Martha was ironing a huge white tablecloth, and the dining table, which was never used (except for jigsaw puzzles), had suddenly doubled in size. Large platters and bowls appeared out of nowhere.

"Biggest travel day in the year," said Martha. "Glad I'm not going anywhere. What sort of a pie would you like?"

"What's the choice?"

"Apple, pumpkin, apple and blueberry or pecan."

"Not pumpkin."

Everyone knew that Martha's turkey never dried out. She conducted a sort of turkey hot line, giving advice: "…then drape it in cheesecloth soaked in butter." Janet heard it twice during breakfast, and was astonished at the quantity of butter.

The big plastic thermometer outside read 26°F. Ned zipped his jacket up to his nose and walked to the bus with a lighter step; a half day of school and no homework. The sun was coming up like a red-purple bruise through the see-through trees, there was a rim of ice around the puddles, and everything had a sparkling edge of frost.

On Thanksgiving Day, Ned woke to the sound of Martha padding around downstairs and good smells rising up from the kitchen. The big turkey had been in the oven since long before dawn. The pies were baked. Everything was ready.

The Rockys crossed First Stream bearing flowers, wine and cider. Ned could hear them laughing before he could see them. Abigail came first, walking backward across the lawn, videoing the others.

"What a beautiful little path," said Viv. "And Martha, it's so *nice* not to have to cook for Thanksgiving."

"That's *exactly* what I was going to say!" said Dave, and everyone laughed.

Viv stood up straight and looked Ned in the eye. "Ned, you're growing so fast, you're morphing!"

After the huge meal and all the talk and the laughter, everyone felt mellow.

"I'm stonkered," Ned announced.

Martha gave him a quizzical look.

"Full," Janet translated.

It had started to rain heavily, and the wind was howling round the house, but they were warm and happy.

"Anyone want to play hearts?" said Abigail, shuffling the cards.

Dave and Martha settled in the kitchen over a second cup of coffee.

"Well now, these boys, what do you think they're up to?" said Dave.

"Ned's on that WebTV every night," said Martha, "and

a lot of other times I don't know about, I'm sure. He's e-mailing around the world."

"To and fro through the woods. They've worn the path clear," said Dave.

"That bear went off the boil pretty fast."

"I think it's to do with a video Abigail made at Halloween. She videoed the same two men at Starbucks."

"Did you ask them who they were?"

"'Just some men.' They're not going to tell us."

"We watch and listen then, I guess," said Martha.

"How's Janet?"

"Doing fine, and Stanley the mechanic's calling about the exhaust next week."

> **Kned**
> **what do you Know?**
> **Knusa**

> **Kuza**
> Thanksgiving there were so many plates of food you couldn't see the tablecloth.
> turkey has white meat and dark meat in case you didn't know and the stuffing had oysters in it (YUUUUKKKK)
> jelly is jello
> cranberries are harvested by flooding
> broccoli is as bad in USA as it is in Oz
> No speeches or singing at Thanksgiving although Martha said Grace
> A boatload of people called the Pilgrims came here (with their servants) to worship in peace. (no TOXIC!)
> The Indians helped them so they cracked an invite to the first Thanksgiving feast

Alakazar worked — I got all the 50 states right
Rocky's making it into A DANCE !
There's one last yellow leaf, hanging on to a branch I can see
from my bed
Here's what I don't know—what to do about Laana
RM

32

Salamander

Yvette Claverloux, along with a hundred and fifty other teenagers, was a weekly boarder at the Abbey School, where she was a quiet star in English and history. She spent the weekends with her Uncle Jérôme at his old house on the river. It was an unusual arrangement, but her parents were away on a two-year posting overseas, and they believed it would be better for Yvette to stay at school in France.

Yvette had been lonely at first, but she found the old stone buildings reassuring, and once she had made some friends, she became part of the large rabble-family of boarders; then it was not so bad when her uncle dropped her off early on Monday mornings.

"Do you miss your parents?" people asked.

"Yes, but we e-mail every weekend."

On Saturday night, while her uncle was watching the soccer, Yvette finished the e-mail to her mother and clicked into the chat rooms. Her uncle's laptop was fast, and she felt like socializing. She liked to pepper her conversation with slang, and sometimes picked up a funny new word from the English chat rooms. Besides, it felt daring to plunge into English chat.

But it was back in Flocon she had the strange encounter of an e-mail kind.

Karma: a le hocquet et s'en va chercher un verre d'eau

Legume_55: c'est la première fois que j'utilise ce webpage

Kuza: HELLo PEEpl es !!! Does anybodylive near a twon called The NAY?

Ikgoo_2D: Légume quel âge as-tu?

Salamandre: Kuza, I live not too far from town Thenay.

Kuza: Any CASTLEs, MANSIONS, VILLAS thaT sort of thing(round Thenay?

Légume_55: j'ai 123 ans et des poussières d'étoile

beeb111: le chocolat, hmm…

Salamandre: Kuza Yes. It is in the valley of Loire river famous for our kings you would say their hunting holiday castles. There is castle in Thenay and big houses but not to view. The castle is private in forest very private behind big gate. Where are you?

Kuza: I am in the NorthernTerritorY in Australia. Are there any UNSUAUAL PETS in Thenay?

Ikgoo_2D: australie ca doit etre cool

beeb111: je ne sais pas, je n'ai plus le contrôle de mes doigts

Salamandre: Do you mean animals pets?

Kuza: Yes

Salamandre: That is a strange question. I do not know. Like snow dogs or horses for carts?

Kuza: Like pythons, CHEEtahs, lions, elephants???

Toxic: Ooo la la Kuza oui oui oui

Kuza: GET LOST TOXIC!!!!!!!!!!!!

The boom of the jet from the air force base nearby drowned out her speech, so Sister Marie-Olivier, the principal of the Abbey School, waited in front of the microphone with the smile frozen on her face until the noise died away.

One hundred and fifty students each held a cake with one candle. It was a festive occasion, and the crowd of parents and onlookers talked and laughed.

Yvette's was a cheesecake. It was hard to see if the candle was still alight. Dominique, beside her, had a more tempting chocolate gâteau. She caught Dominique's eye and grinned.

"For a century and a half the old Abbey has been a school....Stone steps worn by the feet of monks and nuns, now racing feet of modern French children...." Something like that, Sister Marie-Olivier was saying. Thanks to Dominique, Yvette had news for Kuza, but it would have to wait until she could e-mail on Friday night.

Jérôme collected her from the Abbey on Friday afternoon in his yellow Peugeot. The first thing Yvette said to him as she planted a kiss on each cheek was, "Can I e-mail when we get home?"

"Of course."

Jérôme drove fast. He had a catering business providing food for various airlines and always seemed to be in a hurry. He was charming, and people couldn't believe he lived alone. He had married when his company was growing, and the job was very demanding. "How can you be married to someone who isn't there?" said his ex-wife. Jérôme was still driving and flying to meetings everywhere, but each weekend he escaped to the country.

Her uncle's house was called La Poterie and overlooked the Loire River. Below its high banks, the river flowed gently west. There were lines beside La Poterie's front door that marked the height of the floods in 1856 and 1866, when the river must have poured through the kitchen a foot deep. It was impossible to believe there could have been so much water.

Yvette climbed to her little upstairs room and dumped

her bag. At the school, she slept in a cubicle in a dormitory with sixteen other girls, but this room was all hers. You couldn't say it had four walls. The ceiling took the shape of the roof, with the dormer window set into it. Above her little desk was an old mirror, and wedged into its wooden frame was a picture of King François I and his emblem, a salamander.

Yvette plugged in Jérôme's laptop and opened the screen for e-mail and carefully typed the address Kuza had sent.

Dear Kuza,
The Château Thenay is just now sold to some person rich. My friend Dominique brother work there. There is a much new building at the Château.
I will try see for myself any elephants.
Salamandre

On Saturday morning, Yvette opened the shutters and the daylight flooded in. She loved that moment when everything in the room sprang into color. Then she leaned on the windowsill and smelled the morning like an animal. The river was never the same. The islands of pale gray-pink sand moved, grew, and disappeared from week to week.

Saturday morning was always the same: washing, then shopping at the market, followed by lunch at La Rose café. Yvette and Jérôme were good companions. If the other needed time alone, that was fine. Yvette said she was going for a bike ride.

Thenay was too far for her to ride all the way, so she decided to make part of the journey by train. She had no map, only Dominique's instructions, so she would have to ask directions.

While she waited on the platform, holding her bike, a fast train flew through. It wasn't a TGV, the fastest train in Europe, but still Yvette braced herself for the blast of air. When the slower local train pulled in, she stowed her bike and took a window seat in the second carriage. Opposite sat an enormous woman absorbed in a cheap romance. Glasses on her nose, broad bosom, she sat square, her feet planted straight flat on the floor, and licked her finger to turn each page. She reminded Yvette of a hippo. The back of the conductor's jacket, hooked up by the antenna of his mobile phone, looked like a strange sort of tail. Everything reminded her of animals now.

From the train, she rode carefully into the little town, where a car might pop out from a narrow alley or speed round a corner. She locked her bike to a post and surveyed the main street. Yvette chose to enter the cake shop, and she was in luck.

The baker's wife and a customer were deep in wide-eyed revelations, competing for the most astounding slice of gossip.

"And they have ordered éclairs and napoleons and madeleines and trays of petits fours. Raymond will be up all night. What an event! It's for the little girl's birthday."

"Apparently he's quite famous and extremely wealthy."

"Well, he'd have to be, to get his hands on the château. You know what the old count was like. On his deathbed, still squeezing 'em for every sou."

They rolled their eyes in unison and laughed.

A saleswoman asked with her eyebrows if Yvette was ready to be served.

"Still choosing," said Yvette.

The baker's wife quickly turned back to the delicious conversation.

"More money than sense, I say. I mean, it's a beautiful view, but Giscard says the plumbing is from the seventeenth century."

"Alphonse tells me they're turning one of the big halls into a recording studio. Here in sleepy Thenay!"

"Better make it soundproof, or they'll be hearing from old Didier. Even though he's deaf, if old Didier doesn't like 'em, he'll hear them!"

They both laughed heartily.

"Florentine, please."

"Five francs, mademoiselle."

"Merci, madame."

Yvette asked directions at the garage on the edge of the town. "It's quite a hill," the man called after her as she rode off down the avenue of poplars. The hill began when she reached the forest and seemed to rise up forever. The bike didn't have gears, so Yvette was standing on the pedals pushing hard. She wished she had a motor scooter, like Dominique.

A high stone wall with an imposing gate came into view through the trees. Standing by it was a young man. Yvette was embarrassed as he watched her pedaling slowly toward him. He bore a striking resemblance to Dominique; the same long face. There was no doubt he was her brother.

"Pierre?"

"Oui. Bonjour?" He said it as a question.

"Bonjour. I'm Yvette Claverloux. I'm in the same class as Dominique at the Abbey School."

"Well, you'll have to train if you want to make the Tour de France."

They laughed and shook hands.

"Dominique told me about the château. She said you were working here."

"Oui. I'm the mason's apprentice. I'm waiting for a truck that's supposed to be delivering materials." He looked at his watch. "They're late. Have to show 'em where to go."

"What's it like, the château?"

"Beautiful. A mess. There's a view of the Loire from the tower."

"Have you seen the new owners?"

"No. They aren't coming here for a couple of weeks. Their overseer is cracking the whip though, and there's a lot to do. Stone steps, framing windows and doors at the back of the house, and near the forest we're building a stone enclosure."

"What for?"

"Don't know. Goats maybe? Dante Mercer's the new owner. He's a singer in an American band. He's in the movies too. Ever seen him?"

"No."

"Me neither."

"They want a good job, but they want it done fast." He laughed. "My boss, Marcel, is the best mason, but he does things in his own time. There's going to be some drama." He pulled a funny face.

A truck coming from the other direction slowed down. Pierre waved to the driver.

"I'd invite you to have a look, but they're strict about letting people in. Don't want strangers snooping around. That's why they liked the old château. It's out of the way."

"If you find out what they're going to keep in the enclosure, please tell Dominique."

"Sure," said Pierre, swinging up into the cabin of the truck. The driver honked the horn, and the heavy old metal gates creaked open. Yvette didn't hesitate. She slipped in behind the truck without a thought as to how she would get out.

Besides looking for elephants, she wanted to see the château. In the sixteenth century, her favorite king had gone hunting and hawking in the vast oak forests all around.

Keeping out of sight at the edge of the forest, she circumnavigated the château. The facade was imposing, but the back was a different matter. It reminded Yvette of picking a delicious-looking apple, only to find it was rotten. She could see a builder's truck, an electrician's van, two men carrying a pipe, several cars and two trucks. They had a job on their hands.

Yvette had to jump down from the top of the high wall to get out. There was no other way. She sat there, scared, for several minutes until the sound of an approaching car forced her to do something. She steeled herself and remembered her father yelling, "Bend your knees as you land!"

She jumped and fell forward. No harm done. Then she picked up her bike from where it lay in the grass beside the road, faced it downhill, and flew.

33

Suns & Moons

Kate could never remember if it was day for Ned, or night for Yvette, or afternoon for Ja, or morning for Rocky, or even which day, behind or ahead. She was so frustrated. If she could just see it, she could understand it.

She scrounged around the house and found four watches: the green plastic Aeroplane Jelly watch she'd sent away for, her mother's red Swatch, her ordinary watch and her father's that he never wore. She set them on Frenchtime, Massachusettstime, Jamaicantime and the actual time in Wakwak, and she put them all on her right wrist. But it was too hot for wearing four watches—she broke out in a heat rash under the straps.

Determined to solve the problem, she spent an hour lying on her stomach sketching little diagrams with globes, suns, moons, arrows, clocks and boxes. Then she found all the materials and began work. She sat at the kitchen table with one leg tucked under and her face set in concentration, measuring, marking, ruling lines and painting carefully on strong watercolor paper.

Helena was delighted to see Kate sitting on a chair at a table with a pencil in her hand, doing something on paper. She was very curious, but she said nothing and kept her distance, because she knew that the slightest interest from her would be the kiss of death.

Kate was working on an elaborate chart, and when she

finished it, she cut it into strips. The she made four more copies and cut them up too.

"I might show you one day," Kate said to her mother. She scooped it all up, went to her bedroom and shut the door.

34

Bonjour

When Ned, Rocky and Cleverton entered the Kelp Room, they found Kate already there and a decorative banner at the top welcoming a new person. Ned was instantly uneasy.

She should have asked us. The Kelp Room is our secret, and she could wreck it so easily by inviting a nutter. Now she's taking over.

Kuza:%*%*%*%*%%*%*%*%%*%*%*%*%*%*%*%**%*

WELCOME SALAMANDRE

%*%*%%*%*%*%*%*%*%*%*%*%*%*%*%*%*%*%*%%*

(French flag) [I I] [I I] [I I] [I I] [I I][I I]

Remote Man: Is that supposed to be salamanDER? Who is this person?

Kuza: no DRE it's french

Rocky: Is this person french?

Kuza: Yes from near Thenay

Rocky: W O W !

Kuza: There are 2 Thenays in the Atlasand on ly on eof them has a castle That's our Thenay

Remote Man: How can you be so sure.

Kuza: i Guessd

Rocky: How did you find Salamandre?

Kuza: in a french chatROOMm

Remote Man: SERIOUSLY KUZA, YOU'RE TAKING RISKS!

Kuza: don't grwol at ME in CAPITAL LETTERS!!!!!!!!!!!!!!!!!!!!

Remote Man: This person is a total stranger!

Kuza: YOU were a total stranger

Remote Man: what do you know about this person?

Kuza: not much

Salamandre: Excuse me. Nothing except Saturday one week ago I ride my bicycle up the biggest hill to the château looking for an elephant.

Kuza: Welcome SALAMandre!!!

Remote Man: Hello Salamandre. NOBODY SPEAK! Salamandre please tell us about yourself

Salamandre: Who are you?

Kuza: What is this, the BLOODY SPANISHINQUSITION? #*%@%*&U@%$*!

Salamandre: What is this Kelp Room?

Ja: Hello Salamandre I am a boy aged 15 in Jamaica

Kuza: SHUT UP EVERYPONE! Salamdre what did you find out?

Salamandre: The château at Thenay is bought by Dante Mercer it needs much repairs

Rocky: DANTE MERCER! Holy Rock'n'rolly!!!!!!!!!!!!!

Salamandre: Is he famous?

Kuza: Salamandre, EVERYONE IN THE WORLD except you (and mayvbe60 zillion Chinese(.knows who Dante Mercer is, He is BIG NAME famous rocxk moVIE BAD BOY.

Remote Man: any elephants?

Salamandre: No animals just workmen fixing the château plus stone enclosure will be built at the back garden maybe for goats.

Remote Man: Why do you call yourself Salamandre?

Salamandre: History is very interesting to me. The salamandre breathing fire is symbol of my favorite king

Rocky: weird

Salamandre: Yes at school they always say to me "Yvette you are weird."

Ja: They always say "Cleverton you're weird mon" to me!

Remote Man: I can assure you Kate is weird.

Salamandre: Who is Kate?

Kuza: Me

Salamandre: Kuza you are a GIRL?! I am so disappointed. I thought you were a boy. I was already half in love with you.

Kuza: sorry

Ja: I AM A BOY

Remote Man: I AM A BOY TOO

Rocky: I am a raccoon Raccoons are better.

Salamandre: So we are secret room of wierd ones?

Rocky: Yep I guess you could say that

Remote Man: The Kelp Room

Salamandre: What is kelp?

Ja: seaweed

Kuza: okay I have to go to school now. I'll tell you more by email Salamdre. At least Europe and Australia are doing something. Come on America you're the continent this ratbag lives on.

Rocky: Kuza this whole thing is a joke. We can't get near him. We're like a dog in the middle who just keeps jumping round and barking but never gets the ball. I vote we give up.

Kuza: No way!!!!!!!!!!!! We don't want to get the ball. We're going to bite the leg off the man throwing the ball.

Remote Man: If you think you can just look him up in the phone book you come and try Miss Smarty pants Australia. I've tried every way I can think of and I'm scared because he knows where we are.

Kuza: Scared!

Remote Man: Yes I am as a matter of fact. He has people all over the place & for some reason he's interested in this area.

Kuza: Well find ouT

Remote Man: Stuff you Kate.

Salamandre: Goodbye fighting ones. Next time I will be Sal and I will bring delicious food that will make us happy.

Dominique told Yvette her news at lunchtime on Monday. Yvette drummed her fingers nervously on the edge of the desk. Could she wait four days to tell Kuza? Not possible. She began plotting in math (Pythagoras), and by Histoire/Geo (the water cycle) she had a plan.

L'informatique was taught at senior level. The computer lab was in the building on the other side of the playing fields. The only other computers were in the front office, or the cyber café in Tours. No. She'd simply have to make it to the computer lab before the senior school building was locked at four o'clock.

Toward the end of the lesson, Yvette rubbed white chalk powder over her face and hunched her shoulders.

"Madame Roche, I am feeling ill. May I be excused?"

She raced into the computer lab just as Monsieur Genou was turning everything off.

"Please may I send an e-mail, please, please, to my parents? It's urgent."

Monsieur Genou glanced up at the clock on the wall.

"Just two minutes? It's my mother's birthday and I totally forgot. She'll be so upset. I meant to write." She was typing as she pleaded.

"Be quick."

Yvette looked down through the glass bench top to the screen beneath, hurriedly typed the message, the address and pressed send. It disappeared.

"Okay?" asked Monsieur Genou.

"Yes, thank you." Yvette gave him a grateful smile.

As she walked back to get her bread and chocolate, her heart still pounding, Yvette looked up at the bare branches of the oak trees, at the millions of intersecting lines made by the twigs. Had she remembered the address correctly and typed it accurately? What happened to e-mail that went missing?

She needn't have worried. Four hours later, Kate read her message.

Dante Mercer daughter get live young bear for three birthday

35

Surprises

Viv announced at dinner that she was getting a new laptop. Her office was moving, and they were having an equipment upgrade.

"Yes siree!" said Rocky, accidentally flicking spaghetti sauce on his T-shirt, the wall and Abigail's arm.

Rocky's bedroom light flashed, and twenty minutes later Ned was nonchalantly leaning on the kitchen wall saying, "I hear you're getting a lethal little laptop, Mrs. Rocky?"

"What took you so long?" Viv laughed.

"Bees to the honey pot," said Dave.

"Actually, Ned, it's a mighty leap from my old computer. Rocky says you're clever. Help me get up to speed?"

"Sure."

Rocky did his little bird dance. "Provided we can use it."

The laptop was slim and light, yet more powerful than anything Ned had ever touched before.

"Magic!" he crowed, his fingers flying through the command shortcuts. The computer flickered, snapping up patches of information that appeared and disappeared like a modern crystal ball in the hands of a master magician, and the copy from the new printer was as clean as cracks in glass.

Viv, the high-powered executive, sat by gangling Ned, their heads bent over the computer.

"Now, to number pages, Ned, what do I do?"

"Like this, Mrs. Rocky."

"He knows more than the techs at work!" Viv told Dave that night as they sat over a nightcap. "He seems to have a sort of computer sixth sense. He referred to the manual twice. *Twice!* He takes a guess and *tap, tap, tap*, he's right!"

Sister Geneviève gave out the mail after school, while the boarders had their bread and chocolate. Yvette wasn't listening. She was thinking of Thenay, and handed on the long thin packet without realizing it was for her. Then she pretended she knew about it. "Oh, it's the bathing suit I forgot when I was staying with relatives."

"In *Australia?*" said a boy, looking at the stamps.

Yvette shoved the parcel in her pocket and played it cool.

Each night after lights out, Sister Geneviève sat on the chair by the door of the dormitory with her big bunch of keys, waiting for everyone to fall asleep. Yvette lay still for what seemed like hours until at last she heard the nun's footsteps padding away down the corridor. Then, by flashlight, under the covers, she opened the packet. It contained a long rectangular folder covered with fabric of bright green frogs on yellow. From Kuza! Inside were four loose strips with numbers marked on them. The folder had a neat little catch—a loop that slipped over a scarlet bead. Yvette fell asleep with the tangible proof of their strange friendship under her pillow.

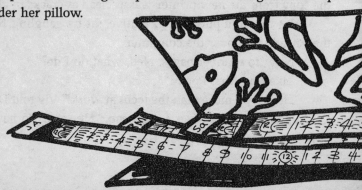

Ned's folder was enclosed with Rocky's, which was just as well because Rocky got home from school first and was able to hide it from Abigail. Besides, if Martha and Janet had seen the packet, they wouldn't have rested until they knew what was in it.

Cleverton's grandmother opened his packet and couldn't fathom it at all. She put it aside until Cleverton came home from school.

"I don't know what you call it," said Cleverton. "It's a sort of time fixer or ready reckoner. You see, this strip is our time in Kingston, this one is for the girl in France, this one is for the girl in Australia and this is for the two boys in America. When we set them together we'll know what time of day it is for each other."

"Whal dat is mose intelligent!" said Hyacinth.

"Yes." Cleverton was delighted, but he didn't tell his grandmother any more, though he had plenty more to tell.

36

Breakthrough

Kuza: <>><<>HELLOEVeryONE<><><<Did you get apacket? Strippy things? Did yours make it, Ja?

Ja: At last, and even my grandmother can understand it

Remote Man: Does your grandmother know about us?

Ja: Not everything

Sal: Very clever Kuza

Remote Man: Brill Kuz!!

Kuza: i=i==i=i=i=i=i okay PeePLES i=i=i=i=i=i=i=i=i=i=i
````````````````````` ATTENTIoN PLEASE!! `````````````````````
)))))))))))))))))))) NOW WE SET THE STRIPS (((((((((((((((((((((((((.
++++++++ sayYOUR time & line 'em up ++++++++++

Remote Man: Masstime Saturday 1pm

Ja: Jamtime Saturday 1pm

Sal: Frogtime Saturday 6pm

Kuza: NTime Sunday 2.30am I'm so KIND to you NOrthern hemisphere guys!!

Rocky: okay All strips lined up and stuck down.

Sal: I want to tell first please

Rocky: GO Salgal

Sal: One American bear cub now is in Thenay, birthday present for Dante Mercer little daughter. She ask for bear toy she get REAL bear too. The stone cage is not for the goats

Rocky: One of the cubs! For sure

Remote Man: Poor bear. We watched them learning to climb. They were so funny.

Sal: No climbing now claws made short

Remote Man: B L OO D Y F R A N K L A A N A !! Bet Mercer paid a mint

Ja: How did you find out Sal?
`````````````````````

Sal: My friend Dominique brother has girlfriend daughter of château cook

Rocky: ************ ATTENTION ************** MY TURN! Mom's work has up-graded her computer. She's got a lethal laptop with THE LOT (but hold the onions - No Games) It's faster than you can think.

Remote Man: The keyboard action is so light it's like talking without moving your lips.

Rocky: I'm using it now.

Kuza: Better than WebTV?

Remote Man: Tortoise

Kuza: Wakeup Ja. YOu alive?

Ja: Awaiting my turn.

Kuza: YOur turn

Ja: Well my friends, I believe we have kept the best until last. What I will tell you is true. You may remember I travelled to my uncle's near Port Antonio which is obviously on the sea. There is a lagoon nearby called the Blue Lagoon, where they made the film The Blue Lagoon. It is very beautiful but for tourists only, because it is very expensive. My cousin, Ermaline, who works at the bar, listened to some customers talking. She thought they were tourists but they were a film crew on a rest day. They were making a movie in a jungle location not far away. Forgive me if I am taking too long.

Kuza: We're reading EVERY litttle leTTER!

Ja: Next day arising early I caught the bus, then walked until I reached the filming. There were many people all working at their various tasks. I stayed at the edge watching, where a man asked me questions about Jamaica. He was a stunt man who had to wait many hours until he was needed later in the afternoon. I became very bold and asked him questions. He knew Frank Laana and once hired equipment from him. All the film people had the most modern phone and communication devices. I grew extremely bold. I said I liked to e-mail friends in America.

Kuza: YOURE KIDFDING!!!

Rocky: You're making this up!

Ja: No I'm not. He wanted to know how I could e-mail. I said my father worked in a hotel.

Kuza: Does he?

Ja: I never met my father. He was a Baptist minister.

Rocky: PLEASE CONTINUE!

Ja: The stunt man had a little electronic notebook in his bag and he gave me.......... are you waiting?

Kuza: FOR GOD"S saek TELL US Before I climd into this COMPUT-ER screen and comedown the tube and STRRRRRRANGLE IT OUT oF YOU!!!!!

Ja: FRANK LAANA'S EMAIL ADDRESS.

Remote Man: W O W !

Kuza: i'm   SPEETCHLESS!!!!!!!!!!!!!!!!

Rocky: YOU WIN JA! No one can top that

Remote Man: KING HIT! Direct to Laana!!

Sal: This Kelp Room feels not real again.

Kuza: you DID make that up!

Ja: No! They asked me to be in the movie. It's called Outside the Circle, I'm the boy who shouts "Look out!" when the truck crashes through the trees. And they paid me $20US.

Kuza: HO HO HO now WHAT????????? What would Hyacinth say?

Ja: When dawg flea bite yuh, yuh haffi scratch

Rocky: Do you understand all this Sal?

Sal: Most yes

Rocky: We need a big fat good idea

Ja: We must be very clever

Kuza: Only On echance!

The Big Fat Good Idea

Ned and Rocky wandered up and down the aisles of the West Concord 5 and 10 cents store, trying to have a good idea. If you couldn't find it in the West Concord 5 and 10, it didn't exist. Their gaze fell on corncob pipes, washboards, crumb catchers, hinges, dog leashes, rat traps, earmuffs, dressmaking scissors, Latin dictionaries and a million other things.

"Nothing," said Ned.

"I *always* have a good idea here," said Rocky. "Have faith."

"How do you do it?"

"Switch your brain to 'Want to Solve Very Badly,' then just mooch, like we're doing, and think lightly, not worriedly. Think like: peppershaker Frank Laana, slime Frank Laana, mohair beanie Frank Laana, rat trap Frank Laana…that kind of thing. You know, anything could be the answer, anything. Just mooch."

Ned picked up a pincushion and was startled when a music box in the base began to play. It played six faltering notes, then stopped. Ned thought he recognized the little tune. He wound it up again. Yes, he knew it. *The Entertainer,* it said on the base. It brought back a simple memory. He was on vacation, in a cabin somewhere, watching a video with his father. Ned listened with his eyes closed. The memory was happy and untainted, as if he was tasting the true flavor of something for the first time.

Rocky was already in the next aisle. Ned let the memory swirl in his mind…his father liked that actor, what was his name?…the spaghetti sauce man…Paul Newman…and that video…? He wound the music box up again and held it to his ear…an idea began to form. The film was about two men who set up a totally pretend place….

"Hey, Rock, ever seen an old movie called *The Sting*?"

"Nope" came the reply from behind the cords, rope and kites.

"I think I might have a big fat good idea."

"What?" Rocky was suddenly there.

"We invent a person." Ned's eyes fell on a sign: GET A GRIP WITH ROLAND FASTENERS.

"Say his name's Roland. We make Roland a customer of Frank Laana's. Roland wants to buy, say, a lizard. Then Laana delivers it to Roland, and we catch him!"

Rocky thought about it for a minute. "That's good!" He appeared to gaze at where the wall met the ceiling. "That's very very good! Rat trap Frank Laana!"

"And to make Roland believable, his business has a Web site," said Ned. "We could do that—set up a proper site and everything."

Rocky, hot with excitement, stripped off his jacket and nearly took off a woman's ear with his arm. "Yes!" he said, whacking Ned with his cap. "That is *definitely* a big fat good idea!"

They went up and down the aisles for another ten minutes, searching for a business for Roland, but they were too excited to mooch successfully. They bought a blow-up globe of the world and rode home on their bikes, tossing the globe to and fro, trying to keep it in the air.

Inventing Roland

Ned e-mailed the big fat good idea to Kate, who read it in an unseasonable heavy storm before the Wet. There's an expression "to run with an idea." Well, Kate did! She ran to Dolobbo through the sheets of gray rain to find out how the Dolobbo Web site was made.

They would always remember the next meeting in the Kelp Room. It was so exciting as each one logged on to the empty screen.

Kuza: How Dee Doo Dee KELP RooMERooMIEs!!!!!!!!!!!!!!!

Rocky: You're looking lovely Kate. That wooden leg suits you

Sal: Bonjour tout le monde. J'ai un grand gâteau de chocolat

Rocky: Pardon?

Sal: hello all the world I have a big chocolate cake

Ja: Good evening & good morning from Sabina Park

Remote Man: G'day

Kuza: Okay Peeples no chitty chat. ~ KNed's hada very <>\<\<\><> Kbig Kfat Kgood Kidea <><><>Tell 'em Kned

Remote Man: We invent Roland, boss of a large successful business. He collects reptiles. We set up Roland's business Web site which looks big deal—warehouse, stressed people, computers, the whole shebang

Rocky: all PRETEND !

Remote Man: Roland e-mails Laana. Orders a lizard. Laana delivers delizard. Got him!

Ja: "We run tings, tings no run we!"

Kuza: Y E S !!!!!! Undestrand Sal?

Sal: We make façade but I am sad because it is all America. What is back side of the business of Roland?

Rocky: Good question.

Kuza: What is the Back side of the busyness of Roland Peeples?

Remote Man: It has to be something we know about so we can talk the talk.

Rocky: Reggae music Ja?

Ja: Yuh askin fe trouble mon! Definitely NO.

Kuza: What arewe good at? Ned, a computr company? Video games?

Remote Man: Roland's not like that. Has to be adult, responsible. Something unusual would be good.

Kuza: Rocky what are you expert at?

Rocky: Taking things to bits

Kuza: The International Taking THings ToBits Company?

Rocky: Sal?

Sal: History of Loire Valley, cloth & costumes of 16 century, François I

Rocky: Expert?

Sal: Yes I have many books.

Rocky: Impressive

Ja: Salamander Imports. European Fabrics of Quality.

Kuza: Hey, that sounds REAL!

Rocky: Cool Ja!

Remote Man: Roland imports fabrics from France. Laana's a stunt man. It won't mean anything to him.

Kuza: What do you think of the name SALamander Sal?

Sal: Roland name his company Salamander because it symbolise patron of good and destruction of bad. It was belief the salamandre live in fire without harm.

Kuza: That's US!!

Rocky: We're on a Roland roll!

Remote Man: What does Roland have in his fridge?

Sal: butter, milk full crème, salmon, coffee, wine, beer

Remote Man: Australian beer, Cascade, cheese

Sal: yes three cheese but not keep in fridge brie, camembert, roquefort

Kuza: Roland's family?

Sal: He marry but divorce. One brother engineer in Africa

Kuza: What does he like?

Sal: movie of Catherine Deneuve, make ski, always whisky Chivas Regal duty free

Kuza: You kknow Roland VERY well!!!!!

Sal: It is my uncle Jérôme.

Remote Man: Car?

Sal: Peugeot 406 coupé, fun car le Cox

Remote Man: What's a le Cox?

Sal: In English I think Beetle?

Ja: But who will make the Web site?

Rocky: Edward

Ja: Who?

Remote Man: me

Ja: Can you do that?

Remote Man: Yes when I find out how

Sal: Difficult! and money!

Kuza: Yes We need a good lookign websit enot some crappyCHucked up thing. RolAnd's got TASTE.

Remote Man: Sal, can you send me a picture of your salamander?

Sal: yes

Kuza: ~~~YOu pig Rocky~~~~ you'v gutszed the chocotlate cake!!!!!!!!!!!!!!!!!

Rocky: YOU only left 2 pieces!

Remote Man: Hey hey What surname for a Roland sort of person?

Rocky: Rock! Roland Rock! Get it! Rock'n' roll, Roland Rock!

Kuza:<>Roland Poland<>Roland Rabbit<>Roland ALONg<>

Ja: Roland Tressel

Remote Man: Odd. Not bad.

Kuza: okay Roland Tressel

Sal: Is this crime? What we are doing?

Rocky: Virtual crime.

Remote Man: Cops get the tip-off on the net, email witnesses, electronic evidence, video conference court case

Ja: But we go to jail in real life!

Kuza: Where does Roland Tressel live?

Remote Man: Massachusetts, near here because we want Laana to deliver to us. For some reason this area is special to him. He lives in LA. How did he know about our bear? Why was he at Starbucks? This is local stuff.

Kuza: What creature does Roland wanf?

Remote Man: An iguana from Jamaica? That okay Ja?

Ja: You are most welcome

Sal: Ja, you speak so old-fashioned English. I like it. I think Roland talk like Ja.

Kuza: ///////,x,x,x,x,xx,x,x,x,x,x,x,x,x,x,x,\\\\\\\\\\
//////////   **ATTNETION!!**   \\\\\\\
I need everybody's besttimes & worst for Klep Room, when home from school, days when not home &holidays JA, library openhours??? Where I fax you in ermergency? Fax for Abbey School SAL??? and you mMUST check email & keep Kelp Room meetigs or or or OR OR~~~
**~~~BAD~~~~~ THINGS~~~~ WILL~~~~~~ HAPPEN
!!!!!!!!!!!!!!!!!!!!!!!!!!!!!!!!!!**

Rock: Are you threatening us?

Kuza: DEFINATLEY ! We are going to catch this SKnuK!

Mom dot com

Having a good idea is one thing. Making it happen is another.

Yvette looked at herself in the mirror and pulled her hair back from her high forehead. She had an old-fashioned face. She was sure Madame Frigo next door thought she was plain and overweight, but Yvette knew if she was corsetted, powdered and gowned she would look for all the world like the Comtesse Gabrielle d'Amboise, who stared down from a painting in the Château de Chambord. And the Comtesse had been a powerful woman in the court of François I.

Ever since coming to live in La Poterie, Yvette had studied the life and costumes of the French court that followed the kings from Paris to the grand castles they built in the valley of the Loire. She reached down her two main reference books and her trusty dog-eared French-English-English-French dictionary. From her bag she took the catalog of fabric from the shop in Tours and a new notebook. Then, relishing the task, she began to draw up lists. Slowly and carefully, Yvette stocked Roland's warehouse with the most sumptuous bolts of the finest fabrics. No expense was even considered.

Yvette worked steadily for an hour, then stretched and smiled at herself in the mirror. How wrong she had been, thinking she would be left out. Her symbol, the salamander, and her knowledge were the basis of Roland's empire. She straightened the picture of the royal emblem. They didn't seem to mind that the scaleless salamander was related to a frog, not a lizard. She imagined a little salamander crawling out of a log thrown on a roaring fire in the hearth of the chambre royale. It was strange, the belief about the creature's mystical powers. She knew that a salamander could not withstand fire.

Then she took her Ready Reckoner from the chest of drawers. The vivid green frogs on yellow could not have been more of a contrast to the tapestry roses on the waistcoat beneath.

"Mom dot com?" Rocky went straight for it. "I have to set up a Web site for school and Ned dot com is helping me dot com do it dot com. Can I use your laptop? Thanks mom dot com you are a brick dot com."

"That's advanced for seventh grade, isn't it?" said Viv.

"Children should be challenged," said Rocky.

"Information technology is the key to the future, Mrs. Rocky," said Ned.

"You're not setting up a porno site, are you?"

Ned was grinning at her too. They made a funny pair.

"Oh, all right, if it won't affect my work."

"No way, Mrs. Rocky."

What difference would it make? She brought her laptop home every night for them anyway.

"What's the site about?"

"Don't know yet."

"Won't it be expensive, a domain name and all that?"

"School's got some deal," Rocky yelled back as he and Ned disappeared up into his room.

Kate was disgruntled. It was partly from lack of sleep, but

also because she felt they were playing a game like chess, in which she was a piece with very limited movement, stuck on the edge. The others were slipping around in the action, and as for Laana, the sneering Mr. Big, he was the black queen with players leaping over each other in all directions.

> **Remotre MOn & Rock**
> **$$$$$$$$$$???? How much is a wedsite?**
> **I'm poor. Ja's poor. SAL? frenCH mony to America. Rock? Please be rich**
> **How do we CATCH LAana? he gets others people to dothe work**
> **WE most have LAANA DE LIVER IGUANA!!!!!!!!!!**
> **We don 'twant some stooge mosuqito shOwing up**
> **NUT NUT NUT hear me nutting. So far nuttin**
> **K**
> **PS Whin the trap is ready I will inform the LAW**

Rocky *knew* he would end up the money man. He took the bear money from under the mattress and laid the two fifty dollar bills side by side. With that and his savings and his pocket money they had a hundred and sixty-seven dollars, which would normally have been a fortune, but Ned thought they needed at least four hundred. He might get money for his birthday, but that was a month away. Besides, it wouldn't be enough.

"I guess I do my little dance at Harvard Square," he said to the cornsnakes.

He offered the Munchkateers a movie deal with popcorn, Coke and the lot, if they went with him the following Sunday. Then, for the first time ever, he practiced his dance, working in some steps from the performers in New York. It felt good.

Egghead

Ned sat like a stunned mullet on the school bus. He didn't notice the color coming into the sky, or the duck that did a skid-landing on the ice at the edge of the pond. He was leading two lives: the school-homework-dinner-bed life with his body, but in his head he lived the Web site, and he couldn't find the right software.

I thought it would be easy to borrow from kids at school. So many parents work in the computer industry, but they don't know what software they've got, or they're reluctant…or something…now if it was a game…

Returning home that afternoon, the school bus churned along the same old route, stopping at the same old stops, the door wheezing open, the goodbyes, the door wheezing closed. Ned didn't even notice the kids laughing up the back. He sat in his usual seat, preoccupied, thinking of how he would anchor parts of the document to the contents. He was cautiously pleased, because in his bag under the seat was the borrowed software. He'd finally tracked it down from Mr. Nichols, the communications teacher.

An earlier generation, but it should be okay. If it doesn't work on Viv's laptop, I'm back to square one. Now I need a scanner. Almost wish I hadn't had that stupid big fat good idea.

They're depending on me. Yvette's designing titles and choosing fonts. Cleverton's writing the words. Haven't seen Rock's new improved making-money dance, but I bet it's good.

Okay, I'll give myself a time limit. Rocky's birthday.

We go home before Christmas. So much to do. I need time and peace and quiet. Oh gosh! Mam's words exactly! Is this how she felt when she crashed? Just keep remembering the bear. We'll get you, Laana.

As the bus lumbered up the straight stretch of Commonwealth Avenue, Ned's eyes focused on a group of people straggling across the road from the car park to the prison. Visitors. He felt sorry for them, having a relative or friend locked up like an animal.

Another person crossed the road, wearing a navy jacket and a brimmed hat. He had a curious walk. Ned sat bolt upright. A limp? Suddenly Ned's mouth was dry. He tried to swallow. He stared at the back of the figure walking along the path to the prison entrance. It was the man they were trying to catch.

Feverishly, Ned zipped up his bag, wrenched it from under the seat and scrambled to the front of the bus.

"Can I get out here?"

"Wait till the next stop," said the driver, surprised to hear this quiet kid speak for the first time.

All the heads in the bus turned to watch Ned as he bolted back along the road with his heavy bag, running as fast as he could toward the prison.

Gasping for breath, Ned reached the imposing stone entrance just as a mother and three children climbed the steps. The kids were somber and slightly resentful, as if they had just been growled at, and the eldest boy was holding the youngest's hand. Ned followed them in. He was reminded of going to see the principal back home: misdemeanors, blame, guilt, punishment. The cold hard sounds of metal and stone.

In a room to the right of the large entrance hall, visitors

sat in a waiting room. People lined up to give their details. Laana was nowhere in sight.

Who's he visiting? Relative? Friend? One of his heavies? You don't visit a jail without a good reason. Client? Smuggling something?

Ned positioned himself with his back to the door where visitors came out. He picked up a newspaper from a seat and hid behind it, sneaking looks from time to time. Others in the waiting room talked quietly, as if they were in church, except for a wild-eyed woman who shrieked at her daughter on a cell phone.

He heard voices and footsteps as a group of people left. He lowered the newspaper to get a better look, but Ned was unlucky. Frank Laana glanced into the waiting room. Their eyes met. A hint of recognition registered on Laana's face, but that was all, and he walked on, out of the building.

Ned was in the New York game again: ever-present danger from any quarter, any time. He had to make a move.

Better to leave with others. Safety in numbers. That old couple.

He followed them. It was dark outside now. Ned was breathing fast.

It's okay. No sign of Laana.

Then the elderly couple climbed into a car at the curb.

He didn't recognize me. I just imagined it. No one here.

The fear subsided a little.

Better get home.

He hurried down the path away from the jail.

Suddenly he was yanked backward by his pack, and an arm caught him around the throat. He lost balance, staggered and was slammed against a tree.

"What do you think you're doing?"

Ned was choking.

"I told you to keep your nose out of other people's business!" said the cold quiet voice.

Ned fought for breath.

"...or you won't *have* a nose to poke in *other people's business!*"

On those words, his head was bashed against the tree trunk and a cluster of stars burst in his brain.

Then the pack was ripped from his back, the vise grip released and Ned slumped to the ground. He crawled around to see Laana swaggering across the road to the car park with the pack in his hand.

The software!

Ned struggled to his feet and stumbled after him.

Tires screaming, the Mustang circled Ned twice; then his bag was tossed into the air like a lump of meat for a dog. Ned hobbled toward it. He was only a few feet away when the car looped around and came at him, hit the bag, spun out of the lot and was gone.

The guard in the northern tower of the prison watched the performance in the lot, impressed by the driving, unaware that the dark heap was a boy.

"I copped one playing baseball." Ned waved his hand at the egg on his head.

"Rocky said you were at the library," cried Janet, grabbing some ice.

"Well, I was; then I played baseball. You're always telling me to join in."

"Oh, Ned, why didn't you call *home*? Why didn't they *help* you?" Janet was supporting him as he struggled upstairs.

"Headache. Don't stress."

Martha tried to pry out more detail.

"Who were you playing with?"

"Kids from school. Can't remember."

"We're not fools, Ned. What's going on?"

Ned closed his eyes.

"Baseball's a *summer* game," fumed Martha as she stumped downstairs.

Rocky ran over after dinner.

"Zounds! That's a lump! You catch a baseball with your *hand*, Edward!"

"I know now."

"Does it hurt?"

"What do you think. Where's M'n'M?"

"In the kitchen. What happened? I said you were in the library. They want me to inform."

"Martha's probably got you bugged. Do me a favor, get my bag. It's behind the chair near the front door."

Rocky produced the broken items from Ned's bag like a series of failed tricks: "The inside of a French textbook. The cover of a French textbook. Squashed lid of pencil case with snake scratched on it…"

"The software, Rock?"

"Gadzooks, Ned, look at it!"

"Oh crap!" Ned punched the bed with both fists.

"Jeepers, Ned. *What happened!*"

"That West Coast cowboy we can never get near."

"Laana?"

"I could smell his aftershave."

"You're kidding?"

"I was sitting in the bus coming up to the prison..." Rocky listened like a cop to a witness's dying words.

"...I'm a gamer, but this was for real. I thought, 'I'm history, but I've got to get the software...'"

"Dang *nabbit*!" said Rocky. "I'm *buying* that software. Stuff scrounging and borrowing. You need the right tools. You're trying to drive a racehorse with a covered wagon hooked on behind."

"What about the money?" said Ned.

"We'll get it," said Rocky. "What's the name of the program?"

"Glass House. It came into the shop last week. When I've finished with it, I'll give it to Mr. Nichols. You'll get it?"

"Honest injun."

Ned closed his eyes, and a look of relief spread over his face.

True to his word, Rocky delivered Glass House the following evening, in its slick plastic wrapping, along with Viv's laptop.

"How you feeling?"

"Thumping headache."

"Why did he have to hit your *head*?" fumed Rocky. "Why couldn't he hit your *leg*? You can keep the laptop tomorrow, Mom's going to Washington. And here's a card from Abigail."

"Groovin'!" said Ned.

"I don't know how I'm going to find the money to get it up and running," said Rocky.

"Mooch in the West Concord 5 and 10."

Ned worked, despite the headaches, stopping only when the screen became a blur. He had headaches for the next two weeks; then he felt better. They never told the others—there was too much going on. Mr. Nichols was delighted to have the brand-new Glass House and let Ned use the scanner in his office.

Four times, Ned took Viv's laptop home to Martha's and worked late into the night when everybody was asleep. But that was hard because he had to run through the woods to return it early next morning, before Viv left for Boston, and then he had to stay awake at school.

On one of these occasions, Janet woke in the night and heard a strange noise coming from Ned's room. It sounded like a soft moth battering itself in an empty cardboard box; silences punctuated by quiet flutterings. She resolved to investigate it the next day, but fell asleep and forgot.

And just when Ned was ready to quit because it was too hard and he was too tired to keep going, this e-mail popped up on the WebTV.

> **Joe**
> George Zilberman makes me write you this story of Laana. I work in the movies, my job a grip. Laana gives me this suitcase

& says get rid of it Now I'm curious I don't throw right then in dumpster, when I have a moment I take a peep. In side— remains of maybe 15 maybe 20 birds but really cant count Terrible mess of heads, leg, bodies all mix in of beautiful ffeathers, red, blue green rainbow. Beautifu birds maybe parrots rare from Austalia I reckon The birds were pack in tubes but drugs wear off they get out of tubes & tear themselfs to pieces Now I am not animal crazy I have dog But still in my head the picture of that terrible thing When people talking Did Laana kill his brother? well I KNOW Laana is cruel NO GOOD You don't reply to me

Salamander Imports

Cleverton was waiting at the door of the library when Winifred arrived. She was feeling silly and spoke in broad Jamaican.

"Where's yuh granmumma?"

"She's coming on the next bus. I brought her bag."

"Gaad amassy, why're you jiggin' like that? You got fleas or somethin'?"

"No," he laughed. "I want to see a new Web site."

"Can a Web site be so excitin'? Me know you into somethin'."

As Winifred switched on the lights, Cleverton turned on the computer and typed in the address. The search seemed to take forever, then there it was.

Salamander Imports. European Fabrics of Quality. His words. Cleverton knew them by heart. He was so proud. The description of the company. Roland's introduction. There was even a photograph of Roland Tressel looking *just* like Roland Tressel! The various departments. A photograph of the building. The catalog of the fabrics with some samples. He went through it word by word. The money order mechanism. He found only one mistake: "courteous" was spelled "curteous." It was brilliant. He wondered if Sal had seen it yet.

"What's this you're looking at?" Ray leaned on the back of Kate's chair and studied the Web site on the screen. "Mmm, pretty fancy fabric, bit different from ours. We couldn't

Salamander Imports

European fabrics of quality

afford a square inch of that stuff. Silk, satin, brocade. Lovely though, isn't it? No wonder they had the French bloody Revolution, with the king's mob prancing round in that gear and others bloody starving. You interested in all this?"

"Yes, as a matter of fact I am," said Kate, clicking back to the home page. "How would you like to be Roland, the boss?"

Ray studied the man's face. "Oh, Roland can have it. He has to be polite to too many people for my liking. Now why'd I come in here? Ah, yes, to get a fish from the freezer."

Kate was inwardly bubbling with satisfaction. When he left, she hugged herself, giggling like a three-year-old.

Yvette ran into the senior school computer room, breathless.

"Another forgotten birthday?" said Monsieur Genou, tapping at a keyboard.

"No, just a little information I need from a Web site. May I?"

"Sure," said Monsieur Genou, without looking up. "I'll be here for the next ten minutes."

Yvette typed in the address and closed her eyes. She didn't want to see the patches as the image assembled; she wanted to see it all complete. When the prickling noises and tickings had stopped, she opened her eyes. It was wonderful! Remote Man had used the pale fabric as a background, as she had suggested, and put the picture of the salamander in an oval. It looked lush and sophisticated.

She clicked on "History of the Company," and there was Jérôme with Roland's signature, which had taken her so long to get right. And the building had an oak tree at the front. The selection of fabrics looked totally convincing, and Ja's words sounded quaintly old-fashioned. She chuckled as she read, "All stock available now…"

"…from the shop in Tours!" she added to herself in English.

"Well, I'm closing up now," said Monsieur Genou. "Find what you wanted?"

"Oui. I certainly did," said Yvette, and she smiled broadly.

E-mail and the Detectives

Kuza: * * WOW !! Wow!! wOW !!!!* * * * America IS RAmPAGING !! * * * * * * fifty people speaking ninty languages all importing like CRAZY!!!! Able to do things FROM AFAR Remotre MAN - YOU havbe done IT !!!!!

Ja: Remarkable!

Remote Man: You sent me the words

Ja: Sal gave me the story

Sal: I wish it is true. I love my collection, all for free. Where the money?

Remote Man: Rocky

Rocky: Aw shucks it was nuthin'. We had some already & I performed a treat

Sal: You are singing?

Rocky: dance

Ja: You must be good

Remote Man: He's cool! Like a magnet. People always stop to watch

Rocky: Rich tourists at Harvard Square

Kuza: so we have Roland & SAL IMP.

Now Roland gets IN TOUCH WITH LAANA

Remote Man: Stay tuned for Ja's draft of Roland's e-mail. I think I can do this

Dear Mr. Laana,
A discreet inquiry. I wish to obtain a Jamaican iguana. Are you able to help me in this matter? A prompt reply would be appreciated.
R T

Ja: Adequate?

Kuza: Great JaBUT I thought a creature from AUSTRALIA

Rocky: very adult words, sounds professional

Sal: little sly feeling is good

Remote Man: send ?

Sal: send

Ja: send

Kuza: A black cockatoo?

Rocky: Jamaica is easier

Kuza: OH ALL rihgt SNED!

Sal: Kuza don't be angry. You are thinking person and encourager

Kuza: BUG DEAL!!!!!!! you thought YOU were remote, Remote, MAn! HA HA HA!!!! TRY being stuck down theback SIDE of the world. I'm sick of setting the alarmn and getting up in the middNDW OF THE NIGHT to listen. If I was there Icould HLEP

Rocky: Don't drama. You're as bad as my sister. You are HLEPPING!

Kuza: shutup

Sal: Before we go. Take a glass please a little drink champagne to my beautiful collection. I am sad too Kuza because now it is all America.

Rocky: chin-chin

Sal: Rocky & RM I always think you are Dupont & Dupond

Kuza: Who?

Sal: In Tintin, two black-suit detectives

Remote Man: Thompson & Thomson! We're NOT LIKE THAT!

Rocky: We wear green suits!

Sal: To iguana catch Laana

Kuza: Ja, you justwant it because it rhymes

Rocky: Glug glug glug I've finished my third glass of champagne

> **Are we toasting or what?**
> Ja: To Salamander Imports
> **Rocky: Salute the compute!!**
> Remote Man: Keep in touch Ja we might need Roland
> Sal: To bears and pythons
> Remote Man: TO KNOCKING OFF BLOODY LAANA

The reply came almost immediately. When Ned saw there was an e-mail, his whole body seemed to buzz.

This is it! We've established communication.

> R T
> **How do you know Laana?**

Snakes alive! Now what do we say? I'll handball it to Kate.

Kate sent an emergency message to Cleverton. Cleverton racked his brains. He desperately needed access to another computer. The library was impossible on school days. After catching two buses, he arrived as it was closing. Besides, even though the others would laugh at how cheap the fares were, he couldn't afford them.

He remembered that the Inter- School Debating Competition was sponsored by Omnet Computer Boutique. Cleverton's team came in second, but the Omnet representative had congratulated Cleverton afterward. Omnet's office was only ten minutes from school. As he walked there he rehearsed his request.

Mr. Orville Daley, a pompous man given to making speeches on "A Bright Future for Jamaica," was very receptive to Cleverton's taking part in the International Youth

Link-Up and suggested that Cleverton should use his computer on Tuesday and Thursday afternoons when he visited clients in May Pen. Mr. Daley already had in mind a new youth slant to his speech. Cleverton was astonished by his success, and couldn't believe how bold he had become.

In the Kelp Room, Kuza and Ja cooked up Roland's reply; then Ja translated from Kuza to English Adult. Ned logged on later, found Roland's message waiting on the screen, copied it and sent it from Salamander Imports.

> Dear Mr. Laana
> Please understand my need for discretion. A mutual acquaintance in the film industry, working in Jamaica, told me of your excellent services. You may wish to visit my Web site—www.salamander.com. My business is mainly with France but I have a special love of Jamaica and species from that island.
> Roland Tressel

> Dear Mr. Tressel
> What a beautiful range of fabrics. I am very interested in your Pompadour brocade. Please send me samples of all the different colors and costs:
> PO Box 2576 Beverly Hills LA CA 90211
> Please don't mention this inquiry to my husband.
> I trust you have large quantities, as it is for curtains.
> I have passed the details of your request to Mr. Laana.
> Maria Laana

An order! Ned's heart sank. "We haven't even made real contact with Laana, and something's gone wrong."

"Come on, Edward. Roland can make an excuse," said Rocky.

"The last thing we want is Maria Laana cheesed off over curtain fabric."

Ned emailed Kate, who set up an emergency meeting in the Kelp Room. Then came the good news, which was also the second helping of bad news.

> RT
> Iguana will cost $5000 up front
> FL

> Ja: $5000!
> Kuza: well peeples, we weren't going to getit for free
> Remote Man: But No Way can we afford that. Unless we rob a bank. I know we're getting criminal but not that criminal!
> Rocky: The first million is the hardest, they say. Give him an IOU? I could dance for five years.
> Kuza: Rem & Rock What's wrong with you guys? That's TOO MUCH!!! BaRGRAIN!!Try to knowck atlEAST$1000 off. Remeber him at Dolobbo Ned? HE bargained. Then say half now, half later. And if he says no deal well at LEAST YOU'VE TRIED.
> PS REMEBER Roland is a good businessman but niCE
> PPs TOugh but nice
> PPps But more touhg than nice
> PPPS A black cOCKAToo would hav ebeen cheaper
> Sal: France is very very pleased for a customer. We supply that beautiful fabric.
> Rocky: What?
> Sal: It is good business
> Remote Man: you're kidding

Sal: No or if you like in french non
Ja: I propose Roland writes:

Dear Mr. Laana
The sum of $4000 was more what I had in mind. I am prepared to make an initial payment of half of that amount. Looking forward to doing a quantity of business with you.
Roland Tressel

"Quantity" is not quite right but I can't think of anything better.
Rocky: Brilliant Ja!! Like that "looking forward to more business" SEND
Remote Man: send

Sal: send
Kuza: sned

Again the reply came swiftly.

RT
OK send Money order $2000 to PO Box 2576 Beverly Hills LaCa 90211
FL

Kuza: FaNTASTric!
Rocky: Yeah, but it's still $2000! In case you hadn't noticed.
Ja: *TWO THOUSAND DOLLARS!!!*
Remote Man: It's impossible. And that's $US We've hit a brick wall.
Kuza: we have NOT
Sal: Non chill

Big Bucks

Yvette went straight to work. She was able to negotiate a good price on the fabric because of the large quantity, and because she and the woman in the shop in Tours shared a passion for silk.

Yvette gave herself an imperious sixteenth-century look in the mirror, crossed her fingers and tripled the price, then she mailed the quote and the samples to Ned, who sent them on with a note from Roland to Maria Laana.

The following Tuesday Yvette was jubilant after the school secretary handed her a fax from her old aunt in Australia. Aunty K said she was getting too old and it was *"definitely curtains for her."* Yvette rang the woman in Tours with a firm order and asked her to wrap the goods well for her to collect on Thursday after school.

Thursday afternoon was gray and windy, but at least it wasn't raining. Francesca, the second cook, lent Yvette her bike, gave her the combination for the lock and told her to be back before she knocked off. Yvette left with the day students and rode quickly along the path beside the river.

When Yvette's parents decided she should attend the Abbey School, they opened a bank account for her in Tours. The account held a significant sum of money, enough for her to buy an airline ticket to Botswana at a moment's notice, and extra for "the unexpected." It was a gamble, but this was certainly the unexpected. Yvette crossed the bridge and rode straight to the bank.

The parcel of fabric was so large and heavy, and the wind gusts so strong, Yvette couldn't balance it and ride at the same time. She set the parcel on the bike seat, held it steady with her elbow and walked as quickly as she could to the post office. Alarmed at how much postage and insurance would bite into her profit, she decided not to send it, and balanced it all the way back to school.

That weekend, she packed it into her middle-sized suitcase and asked Jérôme to mail it from Dallas, Texas, where he was going on business. He was always buying goods in other countries for friends, and bringing things home duty free.

"What is it?"

"Curtain fabric for a friend of my mother's in California." She showed him a swatch.

"Very traditional," said Jérôme, parking the case by the door, ready to go.

"Are curtains expensive?"

Martha looked at Ned quizzically. "Depends if they're ready-made from Target, or top quality fabric made up especially."

"Top quality."

"That's big money. Why the sudden interest in *curtains*?"

"I don't know." Ned shrugged. "Just something I'd never thought of before."

Wow! All this money from Sal—for things that just hang around the place. Amazing. But we still need two hundred bucks. Kate says wait. Rocky's looking for things to sell. So close yet so far.

Ja
Can you transletthis into ENGLISH Adult and emial it back. Sorry in d hurry.
Dear MIdd Bones (excetp we dont know her NAme)
You scored an ace snake x-ray paingting from here (Wakwak) about 4 omnths ago. It;s half of a PAIR the the otherone's gbetter if you ask me. YOu'D lOVE IT. How about you biuy It for $400 by money order?Specal deal
YOurs deserptate,
blablabal

Dear Sir / Madam
The Aboriginal snake painting you were sent from our gallery earlier this year is one of a pair. I believe the second painting is even better than the first. For a limited time, at the special price of US$400, the second painting is available. If you are interested, please forward immediately a money order for that amount.
Sincerely,

Kate typed it slowly, letter by letter, hardly breathing, trying to stop her fingers stampeding as usual. Then she checked it and corrected it and checked it and corrected it, then finally printed it on Dolobbo letterhead, forged Ray's signature, and sent it to Resident at the NY NY address she knew by heart.

And that's how most of the up-front money for the iguana was paid, by Frank Laana himself—for Maria's curtains—with the remainder coming from his very good customer, Miss Bones.

Miss Bones knew Laana had paid $200 for the first painting, but she paid the $400 without complaint. It could have been because that boy in the shirt had liked snakes.

Baiting the Trap

There was e-mail for Salamander Imports each night, but Ned ignored these potential customers. On the eleventh night came the message he was waiting for.

> RT
> Delivery Nov 30 6pm Route 495 Littleton MA 5 miles north of exit 30 parking lot by Donut Shack Courier to recognize you from web pic
> FL

"*Courier!*" The word was like a huge boulder blocking their path. Ned groaned and pushed the laptop away from him.

"Well, the pickup spot is very good," said Rocky, trying to be cheerful. "The Old Tool Shed's up on Route 495, where Dad's buying me a good vise for my birthday. The donut place is kind of isolated, nothing much round but forest, and Dad always stops there for donuts. Always."

"But *courier!*"

"I know."

> Kuza
> We've got the time, the date, the place and Rock thinks his dad will take us.
> It's all there *except* we haven't got bloody LAANA!
> Think us out of this one!
>
> RM

He attached Laana's message.

Kate's face screwed up with anguish. "A courier? NO! NO! NO! We want *him*!" She slapped her leg so hard it hurt. It was all too impossibly far away. She worked herself up to a fury, pounding at the keyboard.

Flatter him.THREATen him.NO DON"t thrEATEN HIM. PROmise him anythig. How can we GET HI m ? What dos he LIKE? MNEY promise hism MNOERY!! MONLEY!! MO NEY!!!!! BLOO D Y FR ANK LAANA!!!! What didMSs HBones say? AnY cleue THERE? M O N E EY
It is TIMe to cnontact the LAW

Getting in touch with the law did not prove easy. Kate thought it would be a simple matter of calling the cops, and if TV was any indication, America was teeming with cops. All she had to do was call, and four police cars would be there on the spot, sirens wailing.

The first thing she discovered was that there were local police for Concord and Acton, then state police for Massachusetts, then federal police for the whole of the USA, and none of them cared a fruit loop about animals.

"You want U.S. Fish and Wildlife Service, Law Enforcement Division," came the reply to her e-mail.

Kate searched the U.S. Fish and Wildlife to find there were five fish and wildlife agents in the whole of Massachusetts: one was on extended leave, another tied up as a witness in a court case in Boston, and the other three were "out in the field." To make matters worse, the division had recently moved its office.

Cleverton and Hyacinth lived in two rooms at the back of an old house near Half Way Tree. The place wasn't much to look at, but Hyacinth liked it. "No every ting wha' got sugar ar sweet." In the hurricane season, the roof didn't leak.

Cleverton slept in the main room, and his bed doubled as a seat during the day.

There were few decorations: Bob Marley, Jesus, a couple of photos in frames, and a little drawing of Anancy the Jamaican spider trickster done by Cleverton when he was ten.

"I have to be cunning like you tonight, Anancy," he said, finding the empty pages at the end of an old schoolbook and folding it back. Cleverton sat down on the doorstep where the light shone from inside. He began to write with the only thing he had of his father's, a mechanical pencil.

Cleverton could hear six muted conversations, reggae from three directions, crickets, frogs, a croaking lizard, night birds and the baby next door crying, but Ja's last letter from Roland was something Anancy would be proud of.

Dear Mr. Laana
I am delighted with arrangements. They suit me well. I am keen to place with you a further order, which, of course, demands a high degree of secrecy. It concerns reptiles from South East Asia. I believe it will prove extremely lucrative for you and I desire to discuss it with you in person. I suggest that you make this delivery so that I can outline the project to you, as I will be leaving for Europe at the beginning of December.
Roland Tressel

Send. **Send.** Send **SmEd**

Day after day they waited for a reply but heard nothing.

> **RM & R**
> He's in! He's IN ! No news it GOOD! It means he's IN, otherwise
> he'd tell Roland, I'm sure. He wans ttheBIGMONEY.'
> K

Not@home

"Sit down please, Ned, we want to have a word with you." Janet and Martha were acting like two judges, the newspaper spread like evidence before them on the table.

What do they know?

"Ned, we hardly see you these days. You're always off somewhere, plotting who knows what. You and Rocky are as thick as thieves." Janet tapped a photo of some teenagers in the newspaper. "This is a shocking story. These kids took off without adult supervision and things got seriously out of hand. Two people were injured."

"It's okay. I've been at Rocky's," said Ned. "We're planning a bit of an event for his birthday."

"We'll look forward to that." Judge Martha studied him over her glasses, unconvinced.

"I don't mind you going off and doing things," continued Janet, "but there's one thing I absolutely insist on. You must always tell us where you—"

Janet was interrupted by a knock at the front door. Martha went to open it.

"My sainted *aunt*!" cried Martha.

"No, I'm not!" laughed a familiar voice; then through the door walked Kate. Hair like an old toothbrush, bedraggled, tired and shivering, she grinned at Ned triumphantly.

"Hello, America!"

"Sometimes that kid drives me right up the flamin' wall!"

Ray slammed the fridge door, and all the magnets fell off.

Helena had the phone clamped to her ear. In exasperation, she waved at him to shut up.

"Just ask him!" yelled Ray.

"Did you dare her, Ned?"

"He says she says she dared herself," relayed Helena.

"Unbloodybelievable!"

"No, we weren't worried," said Helena. "Not in the slightest. Until two minutes ago, we thought she was at a sleepover in Darwin."

Ray raged on. "How did she pay for it? We'll be borrowing money from the bloody tooth fairy, the way we're going."

"Ned says she'll talk to us in half an hour, when you've simmered down."

Helena hung up the phone and scratched her head fiercely with both hands. "And I have to *live* with you two!" She plomped herself at the table. "Well, there it is. A long weekend sleepover in Darwin turns out to be a sleepover in the USA. It's all that e-mail. I knew they were up to something."

"Where'd she get the passport?"

"For Bali, remember."

"That was four years ago."

"Still current."

"What about permissions, visas? She can't just get up and go."

Helena sighed. "'Member those forms, medical things, some permission we signed? Couple of weeks ago? Pen pals, or camp or something? 'Member?"

"How, in the whole of bloody King Kong's kingdom,

did she pay for it? That girl's going to give us the whole box and dice."

"She's on the other side of the world, Ray. You can't make her do anything."

"Sleepovers! They can forget bloody sleepovers. They're never going to sleep again!"

Helena and Ray sat on either side of the table in stunned silence, just the sound of the air conditioner battling to keep out the natural temperature of the place.

"Business class!" sighed Ray. His mouth twitched at the corners, then gave way to a chuckle. Then he threw back his head in a roaring laugh. "A relative of mine flew *business* class. Now *that's* a first."

Janet hadn't seen Kate since she was seven. She looked at her niece, bemused. She was the living mixture of her lovely sister and the cranky man she married.

Kate vehemently insisted she was given a ticket by American Express and that she was there for Rocky's birthday party. She refused to say more.

"This is obviously going to be quite an event," said Martha. "How do you know Rocky?"

"By e-mail. And I wanted to see you, and the beautiful autumn and everything," she said innocently. It didn't fool anyone.

She tried another tack. "Stranger things happen at sea, you know."

Officer Dekker of Fish and Wildlife was umpiring between

humans and beavers in Groton when Kate finally tracked him down. She didn't waste words. Dekker didn't know what to make of this girl with a strong Australian accent, but by the third phone call, whether he believed her or not, he was getting pretty sick of her.

Her story was like a bad movie script, but a couple of things rang true. He knew about the bear shot in the forest, and there had been reports of early-morning flights from Stow airport. Why did this have to happen when they were so short-staffed?

Kate wriggled and itched and scratched like a dog in the unfamiliar hot bedding on the mattress, catching fleeting patches of sleep, envious of Ned's slow steady breathing, listening to the noises of the house and the faint roar of the furnace, and hoping like mad that Officer Dekker would get it right. Tomorrow was Iguana Day.

Iguana Day

```
##########################################
[ X ]                                  [ X ]
::::*REMOTE MON *:::G  O  O  D   L U CK ::::* ROCKY MON*:::
[ X ]                                  [ X ]
##########################################
```
[II] Que la force soit avec vous! [II]

Even though they were early, Ned and Kate ran down the path through the forest. This was not a time to be late. Then, stepping across First Stream, they heard a shout—and there was Rocky, flapping toward them like a wounded pelican. Eyes wide, gasping, he stabbed his glasses back on his nose. "Dad can't take us!"

"Oh, *WHAT*?"

"One of his best customers wants his car tonight."

"Oh *NO*! We'd need a miracle now," said Ned.

"Laana will still be caught," said Rocky apologetically. "We just won't be there...."

"Like hell we won't!" said Kate. "A taxi! Hitchhike! The bikes! Call your dad again. Try him one more time."

"You promised, Dad, you *promised*!"

Dave was speaking loudly, under pressure. "I know, son, I'm sorry, but just occasionally this sort of thing happens. Look, I've got to make a living here, you know."

"You agreed to it ages ago. Ned and Kate are waiting. Today was the day."

"Grow up, son. You're carrying on as if it's the end of the world."

"We're just very disappointed."

"Are you at home?"

"Martha's."

"Janet there?"

"Yes."

"Put her on."

"Hi, Jan, can you take them to the Old Tool Shed in Littleton?"

"Fine, Dave. No problem." She hung up. "Let's go," she said brightly.

The three looked dumbstruck.

"It's okay, the Hunk'o'junk is capable of carrying four, you know."

"Great!" said Kate as if breaking a spell. "Let's go."

Ned slipped into the passenger seat.

What are we doing? Too much happening. Too much on the hard drive. Overload. I can't process things quickly enough.

The Hunk'o'junk sounded like a 747 taking off. Third gear and top were bad, but first and second were deafening.

"It's *WORSE*!" Ned shouted to Janet.

"Yes, and I must be *BETTER* because I don't *MIND* so much," she yelled back. "It's the exhaust. We'll be *FINE* as long as we don't see a *COP*! The mechanic's going to fix it *NEXT WEEK*."

There was no chance to talk. Ned glanced at Rocky and Kate in the back seat. Kate shrugged. Ned shouted directions above the roar. They were twenty minutes down the highway when Rocky leaned forward and yelled, *"Dad always*

STOPS FOR DONUTS at the DONUT SHACK UP AHEAD. LET'S STOP FOR DONUTS."

"*GREAT IDEA!*" yelled Kate.

"*WHAT TIME does the OLD TOOL SHED CLOSE?*" yelled Janet.

"*LATE. LOADS OF TIME,*" yelled Rocky.

The neon sign above the run-down wooden building read ONUTS. Occasionally the D flickered on. They swung into the parking lot. "*DAD always parks UP PAST THE SHACK. PARK UP THERE.*"

They stopped and Janet laughed in the blissful silence. "Boy, family tradition sure runs strong in your family, Rocky."

"Yes, especially with donuts and birthdays, Mrs. Ned," said Rocky in an excessively cheerful voice.

The overcast day had darkened to night, and the yellow light from the Donut Shack lit five cars. A station wagon pulled in and a family burst out. Not one of the customers looked like a Fish and Wildlife officer.

They ate the first bag of donuts slowly, scanning the highway, stamping their feet to keep warm.

"Mmm, great donuts," said Rocky.

Several cars passed. No one came or left the parking lot. Time crawled by. Ned felt as if a steel spring was tightening in his chest.

"Great donuts," said Kate.

"I feel really hungry. Let's get some more," said Rocky.

"We can eat them while we go," said Janet.

"Oh, Dad never drives while we're eating donuts. Doesn't want to get the car sticky."

"Not a problem with the Hunk'o'junk," laughed Janet.

"Oh, I wouldn't want to risk it, Mrs. Ned."

The noisy family piled back into their car and drove off. Rocky bought more donuts.

Two more cars and a truck pulled in, but no one looked like an Officer Dekker.

"Where *is* he?" hissed Kate.

It was ridiculous. They couldn't eat another donut, but Rocky kept buying more.

"Well, I'm going to wait in the car," said Janet, slightly annoyed. "It's too cold to stand around out here. When you're thoroughly stuffed with donuts, we'll go."

Ned, Kate, and Rocky watched the highway through the windows of a van. In the pale light from the Shack they looked sallow, and the forest full of menace. Then headlights pulled off the highway, cruised toward them and parked just beyond the circle of light from the building.

"The Mustang."

"*Yes!*"

That car again. The feeling in Ned's chest grew tighter.

The dark shape of the vehicle was sinister, like an animal waiting to pounce. They could make out a speck of light. Cigarette. The driver was waiting; they were waiting; Janet was sitting in the car waiting.

"I'm sure it's him," whispered Ned.

"I can't *stand* this," hissed Kate. "Where *are* you, Dekker?"

"The iguana will be on the backseat, warm."

The seconds dragged on.

"Damn! Why doesn't Dekker come?"

At that moment, another car left the highway and rolled into the parking lot. The door of the Mustang opened.

"Come on, man, get out of the car," said Rocky.

"The Cowboy!"

"*Yes!*" squeaked Kate. "We *did* it!"

"Shut *up*! We haven't *done* it! He drives off and it's all over. We don't even have *evidence*."

Laana stepped away from the Mustang and stretched, glancing at the driver's window of the other car.

"He thinks it's *Roland*," hissed Kate. "He's remembering the Web site photo."

Then a short balding man climbed out of the other car, zipped up his jacket and strode past him to the Donut Shack.

"What's going *on*?"

"Dekker?"

"Don't…think so."

Laana watched the other man, checked the time, and climbed back into the Mustang. The seconds dragged by. Three cars left and another drove up and parked close to the Shack. Two women. Laana got out of the car again and flicked something from the windscreen. He looked around and went to climb back in, but changed his mind and walked into the shadows of the forest to relieve himself.

"Where's *Dekker*? We're going to *lose* him," hissed Rocky. "When he gets in this time he'll drive off."

"I can't stand this!" said Kate.

"Mam'll come looking soon…," said Ned. "The iguana?"

They took their chance. Crouched over, they ran to the Mustang. Kate held the door as Ned and Rocky juggled the box from the backseat. It was long and heavy and the car was low. Something scuffled inside it. Struggling with the box, they ran awkwardly past the Donut Shack, and piled into the Chevy.

"*GO, MAM, GO!*" Ned shrieked.

"WHAT'S HAPPENING?"

"FLOOR IT!"

Janet saw the wild urgency in their faces and swung out on the highway. She missed second gear and jumped straight to third with a roar.

"DID YOU STEAL DONUTS?"

"NO."

"WHAT THEN?"

"A MANIAC!"

"SEAT BELTS!"

"CAN IT GO FASTER?" yelled Rocky.

"FLAT TO THE FLOOR!"

The Hunk'o'junk thundered on. Kate felt sick, ready to explode with disappointment, fury and donuts. Janet was spooked, wide-eyed.

"WHAT'S IN THE BOX?"

"IGUANA!"

They battered along the highway for a mile, before the headlights loomed up behind them. It could have been any car, but it drew closer and closer until the lights were blinding, shining in like a UFO encounter.

"WHAT ON EARTH...NED?" shrieked Janet.

Suddenly they were rammed from behind. The Chevy jolted forward like an amusement park ride. The seat belts cut into them as they lurched violently. They screamed. On the second jolt, Kate vomited donut all over the iguana box.

Then, with a roar that they could hear above the thunder of the Hunk'o'junk, the Mustang shot past them, streaked up the highway and disappeared. Other cars drove by, oblivious to the drama.

"*NED, I WANT TO STOP! IT'S A MADMAN!*"

"*NO, TAKE THE NEXT EXIT!*"

Please give us the exit, we're sitting ducks.

But the blackness of the forest continued on either side. Ned knew it wasn't the end of the game.

A moment later, Ned saw headlights in the distance, coming toward them. They seemed to be on the wrong side of the highway. Then they disappeared as the road dipped down. A few other cars passed them but Ned felt a cold hollow feeling of fear.

The headlights reappeared closer, *much* closer now. They *were* on the *same* road, he was sure of it, traveling fast. Laana was heading *south* toward them on the *northbound* side of the divided highway!

"*OHMYGODOHMYGOD!*" Janet moaned. She switched to the left lane. The lights switched to the left lane. She swung to the right, they followed her. Like eyes staring them down, getting closer every second.

"*NED, I CAN'T SEE! OH GOD! HELP ME!*"

Ned's mouth was dry. He scrambled for the sunglasses. They were useless. A head-on collision! He felt dizzy, awash with fear.

Rocky reached from the back, snatched the glasses, broke them and put one lens over the other. "*TRY THAT!*"

"*NED, WHAT DO I DO?*" Janet screamed, her hands welded to the steering wheel.

He opened his mouth. He couldn't speak.

"*NED?*" she screamed. "*NED?*"

It's like staring at the sun. It's like...a Laana movie! The stunt in Fray! *He's setting us up! So it's a stunt, is it? Well, I play games too.*

Suddenly Ned found his voice. "KEEP IT STEADY, MAM," he yelled. *"GOOD DRIVING. SAME SPEED, STAY IN THE CENTER LANE. GOOD DRIVING."* He yelled continually. She focused on his voice, as if hypnotized. *"STRAIGHT AHEAD. KEEP STEADY."* Fear squeezed his heart but he kept on. *"KEEP STEADY, GOOD DRIVING."* The lights were blinding. *"SHUT YOUR EYES, MAM!"* he screamed above the Chevy's roar. Somehow, squinting through the lenses and his sleeve, he could see. He was the eyes for them all. *"SAME SPEED. STRAIGHT AHEAD. KEEP STEADY!"*

A fraction more, or less for her overreaction?

"GOOD DRIVING. KEEP STEADY," he screamed. *"WHEN I TELL YOU, TURN AN INCH TO THE LEFT."* He glanced across. Her eyes were shut. *"GET READY."*

Wait till it feels like too late.

"NOW!"

In a blinding flash and a scream of tires, they swerved just as Laana swerved.

"MISSED!"

The Chevy rocked wildly with the rush of air, but kept its course.

An inch, I swear!

"OPEN YOUR EYES, MAM."

Kate twisted round to look behind. *"HE JUST PASSED A TRUCK. HEAR THE HORN!"*

"HE'S DOING A U-IE!" screamed Rocky.

"THERE'S A POLICE CAR AT THAT PULL-OFF! PULL IN THERE!"

"CAN'T!" cried Mam. *"GOING TOO FAST!"*

But the policeman at the pull-off heard the roar of the

Hunk'o'junk. Carefully, he put his coffee in the coffee holder, swung in behind the wheel, radioed the station and gave chase. He was just picking up speed when he was overtaken by a Mustang flying like a rocket.

"HE'S COMING UP BEHIND US AGAIN," screamed Kate. "OH GOD, HE'S COMING SO FAST!"

Laana was between them and the police car.

"NED?"

Suddenly there was a thunderous tearing and scraping of metal, a crash and a jolt—and the din of the Chevy doubled.

"MY GOD, WHAT WAS THAT?"

"THE EXHAUST'S FALLEN OFF!"

Maybe, when the Hunk'o'junk's exhaust hit the Mustang, Laana was way past caring. Maybe he did fight to control the car. Nobody knows. But he wasn't the type to panic.

Frank Laana's last stunt was witnessed by Rocky and Kate through the back window, by Ned in the rearview mirror and by Officer O'Reilly as he swerved wildly to avoid collision. The event was recorded only in their memories, but as a stunt it was Laana's masterpiece.

The car lipped up the barrier at the side of the road, flipped and flipped again, tumbled and spun like a child's toy, its lights flashing wildly around the highway, the forest and the night sky.

"GOD ALMIGHTY!"

Janet didn't see it. Her eyes were on the road and every breath was a whimpered cry. All she could hear was Ned chanting, "KEEP STEADY, MAM. GOOD DRIVING."

And so they drove away from the horror. They dipped down a hill, rounded a gentle curve and then the road straightened out. Just the lights of the Hunk'o'junk pushing into the darkness. They were roaring down the highway, alone.

"THAT HAPPENED, DIDN'T IT?" yelled Kate, deathly white beneath her tan. She could feel the iguana scrambling in the box.

"BET YOUR LIFE IT DID!" yelled Rocky.

"GOD, I LOVE THIS STUPID CAR!" Ned's whole body was shaking.

The Oak Motor Inn

At last, the exit sign loomed up. They rolled into the first place where they could pull off the road, which happened to be the driveway of the Oak Motor Inn. They were all in a bad way. Janet, white as a ghost, was breathing unevenly, her teeth chattering. The Hunk'o'junk stank, and the air outside was freezing cold.

"I think I'm going to chuck again." Kate blundered out of the car, but instead of making for the bushes she stumbled to the motel lobby, then tottered back, waving a key.

"S-seven," she bleated.

Janet made it to the room leaning on Ned, her legs barely able to support her. With a heavy heart he helped her onto the bed and took off her shoes as he'd done once before. She lay shivering with her eyes closed.

Oh God, how far have we set her back?

Rocky struggled in, carrying the box with the iguana. Kate was making disgusting noises in the bathroom. Disgusting smells.

"H-h-hurry *up Kate!*" Rocky was desperate too.

Although the room was beautifully warm, they were all shivering uncontrollably. Ned wrapped Janet in a comforter and massaged her frozen hands.

"Who...who was that?" she asked.

Rocky called from the bathroom.

"T-tell you later," said Ned.

Rocky had the lid off the box. The iguana, a beautiful majestic creature, was like an old man who should have flown first class but was bundled onto a freight train. The last quarter of his tail had been bent around to fit in the box. Carefully, they lifted him onto the floor, where he slipped around pathetically.

"Oh *NO*! L-look, he can't w-walk properly!"

"S-something's wrong with his leg!"

"Put him b-back so he can't hurt himself any more."

Oh God! We've caused nothing but trouble.

Ned suddenly felt his legs might buckle. He followed Kate's example, wrapped himself up and lay on the floor. Rocky did the same.

"D-d-death-defying, Edward," croaked Rocky; then silence fell.

It was broken by a knock on the door. Mr. Maitland, the owner of the motel, entered with two U.S. Fish and Wildlife Division of Law Enforcement officers, Dekker and Horst. Dekker was the balding man from the Donut Shack. In the bright light he looked honest, and Ned felt he could trust him with the iguana.

"M-Mr. D-Dekker, the iguana in the b-bathroom can't walk p-properly," said Ned.

"M-Mr. D-Dekker, w-why didn't you arrest L-Laana?" shivered Kate.

"Horst, check the iguana. You Kate?" Dekker addressed the bundle near the bed that moved. "Thought it was you. Saw you kids by the van."

Then a police siren wailed up and they were joined by a state police officer, Officer O'Reilly, and local police officers Muir and Corrow. Mr. Maitland, who had a crumb at the corner of his mouth through the whole proceedings, sent his son to fetch more chairs.

It was a strange scene: a small motel room with four

shivering bodies cocooned in comforters and blankets being questioned by five men, all trying to get their facts straight for their particular slice of the law, between calls on the radio and beepers beeping.

"Iguana's got a dislocated shoulder."

"Narcotics?" O'Reilly snapped into his radio. "Well, nobody's gonna get to question him. He's not gonna answer!"

Mr. Maitland's son brought hot coffee and donuts.

"Uggh! *D-donuts!*" said Kate. "I'm never going to eat another d-donut for the rest of my life!"

There was some debate about official statements; then two tape recorders were set on the table. Officer Dekker took a deep breath and said quietly, "Now who's going to tell us what happened?"

"A-actually it starts in Australia," said Ned. "Y-you tell it, K-Kate, and R-Rock and I'll interrupt."

Things went fine till Kate skipped to the chase. "You should have *caught* him!"

"The job was in *our* hands," said Dekker. "Why didn't you leave it to the law? We wanted to get the rest of the gang and that other guy too, Tressel."

"No, that's *us!*" Kate exclaimed, throwing back the doona. "*W-we* are Roland Tressel."

"No, this Roland Tressel's got a big import company. Been collecting animals for years."

"That's *us!*" said Kate, practically crying with exasperation. "I told you. We *invented* him."

"Pardon?"

"*Who's* Tressel?" said Constable Muir.

"Actually, he's Yvette's uncle J-Jérôme. You see, there are actually two other people involved."

"In Massachusetts?"

"Actually, Y-Yvette's in France and Cleverton's in J-Jamaica."

O'Reilly turned to Dekker. "This story has more actuallys than I've had hot dinners."

The tale the kids told was long, convoluted and fanciful, yet they were so insistent, all agreeing and chipping in details, that the officers found themselves believing it. No one could possibly invent such a story, then act it out so well.

"Sounds freaky, but it's true, honest injun," said Rocky.

"Were you aware of all this, ma'am?"

Ned turned to look at Janet behind him. He'd forgotten about her. She was sitting up now, listening intently.

"No," said Janet. "I'm fascinated."

"Why are you in America?"

Ned watched her closely.

"I was ill," said Janet. "We came here for me to recover." Even after that terrible drive, she said it as if it were history.

"Ma'am, were you aware that you were speeding in an unroadworthy vehicle, endangering lives?"

Ned felt guilty. He glanced up. All faces were serious. Janet chose her words carefully. "I think the outcome might have been…very different if our exhaust hadn't fallen off."

"Ma'am, did you know your son was so concerned about animals?"

"Oh yes, he's passionate. He keeps lizards at home. He can watch reptiles endlessly."

"Could he set up a Web site?"

"If he wanted to."

"You kids have any background on Laana?"

246

Rocky looked at Ned. "A whole heap, and videos."

O'Reilly shook his head in disbelief.

"Yeah, this is one out of the box," grinned Dekker.

"Do you think the good things balance out the bad things?" asked Kate.

"We're getting the facts," said Dekker.

"Can I ask a question?" Ned turned to O'Reilly. "He's dead, isn't he?"

O'Reilly nodded. "A fatal."

"Did you see it?"

If there was one cop in the whole of the Massachusetts police force best suited to tell of Laana's last stunt, Officer O'Reilly was the man. He had recently completed an advanced skills driving course so he knew the jargon, he had a calm deep voice and a way with words.

They heard it first in the Oak Motor Inn, room seven, but O'Reilly's account appeared in all the local papers and *The Boston Globe* on the East Coast, accompanied by a photograph of what was left of the Mustang. On the West Coast, the *Los Angeles Times* printed it with a couple of sensational stunt shots, plus one of Frank and his wife, Maria, in happier days.

In Hollywood, that bizarre city of manufactured dreams, the stunt industry obituary, under the heading "Driver and Car Were One," carefully pieced together the trajectory of the Mustang. And somehow they deduced that Laana hadn't been wearing a seat belt.

The Mustang was triple shrink-wrapped and flown west, where Frank Laana was buried in his car.

Wah happen?

Ja: Did we catch him?

Rocky: No

Kuza: Yes

Remote Man: Let me tell it. I can't get it out of my mind. Mam drove us to the Donut Shack in our old Chevy where we waited ages. Then the Mustang cruised up.

Kuza: It was him alright

Rocky: The bait worked Ja. He was hungry for the deal.

Remote Man: He sat in the car and we waited & waited & waited for Fish &Wildlife to do something.

Kuza: It was so bad

Ja: How do you know Kuza?

Kuza: I was there.

Sal: You joke?

Rocky: No She's here. We're sharing the keyboard

Remote Man: Let me finish. We thought we would lose him completely so we made a dash for the iguana, took it and bolted in the Chevy.

Kuza: Laana chased us

Remote Man: I have never been so scared. First Laana rammed us then he drove straight at us. It was nearly a head on.

Kuza: Ned's mum drove like a robot

Rocky: Ned told her what to do.

Remote Man: I remembered his movie Fray where he clips an on-coming car. It spins out of control and he gets away. Then he was coming up behind us again

Rocky: B U T

Kuza: Our exhaust fell off and hit him!!!!!!

Remote Man: The Mustang bounced around like a rubber car and crashed.

Sal: Frank Laana is dead?

Remote Man: Yes.

Rocky: The Mustang was a write-off Looked like a block of uncooked noodles

Ja: Did we kill a man?

Remote Man: I don't know Ja.

Kuza: He DEFINiTELY tried to kill us!!!!!

Remote Man: My mother is back on medication again but I think she's sleeping better than me.

Sal: The iguana?

Rocky: He's magnificent. So beautiful. He scored a dislocated shoulder. Fish & Wildlife took him.

Sal: This is not how I think it will be. Not so happy

Kuza: It was terrifying

Remote Man: Every time I close my eyes I see those headlights

Kuza: We were centimeters from being cactus

Sal: What do you mean?

Kuza: You would be waiting here, Sal, and we would never log on

Rocky's Party

Janet, Martha, Ned and Kate were met on the track by Abigail, with the camera to her eye, commentating continuously. Ever since the plan to catch Laana, which was now known as "The Entrapment," she had become a reporter.

"Here come the Australian adventurers from Melbourne, herpetologist hero Edward Spinner, and his famous scientist mother driving ace, Janet, and Kate Out-of-nowhere, who's flying home tomorrow, lowest class, and our last guest, Martha B. Sudbury, champ turkey-roaster. They are coming out of the forest now, moving up the path to the birthday party of Cabot 'Rocky' Brotherbum, which is also a goodbye party for the Aussies who are shortly to return home, when they've packed up their junk and sold their hunk'o'junk."

"Enough, Abby," said Dave.

"Welcome, everyone," said Viv.

It was such a happy sad time. Beneath the lighthearted surface of the party swirled deep undercurrents of emotion. Jokes were funnier, sad things sadder, odd things strangely moving and poetic. It was almost as if they were all drunk on each other's company, or their luck at being together, of being alive, after the terrifying events of the day before. Kate was shy for about two and a half minutes, and Abigail fastened onto her as if she'd found the Messiah.

Jade and Kari dropped in briefly so the Munchkateers could present Ned with a special goodbye video. In it they were snake people and everything they said started with an S. It was typically extraordinary and funny.

Then Rocky blew out the fourteen candles on his ice-cream cake, and Dave staggered in with his present. Everyone laughed because they knew it was a vise.

"So you made it to the Old Tool Shed?"

"Different in daylight. Ordinary."

"We didn't stop for donuts," said Dave.

"I don't *do* donuts," said Kate with a pained look.

"I'm sorry, but I can't talk about that drive yet," said Janet.

They changed the subject.

"Kate, you're like a meteor that crashed to earth in Concord. We all want to know how you got the plane ticket."

Kate looked coy, a tuft of hair over her left ear. "Okay, since you're all so desperate, I'll tell you." She folded her arms. "I have a sponsor."

"What?"

"Lots of people have sponsors. It's nothing unusual."

"No offense, Kate, but why would someone sponsor you?" said Rocky.

"Because I'm beautiful." Nobody believed that.

"Give us the 'actually,'" said Dave.

"Well, actually"—she paused and frowned—"I've *lost* my sponsor."

"*Laana?*"

"Yep."

"How on earth?"

"Well, you know the second X-ray snake painting?"

"This sounds a bit criminal," said Rocky.

"A little," said Kate. "The old lady paid *me* for it, and Laana paid Dolobbo. In the pile of credit card forms at Dolobbo I found the one for when he bought the first painting by phone; then later, on a new form I just copied it using the same numbers, and stuck it in the pile with the other forms. No problem."

Everyone stared at her. The adults were clearly horrified.

"So then... he bought me the plane ticket."

"Kate! You don't just go flying around the world like a rich hippie on someone else's credit card. People go to jail for that!" said Janet, shaking her head in disbelief.

"I've only done it *once*, and it was *Laana's* credit card."

There was silence except for the adults breathing heavily.

"Sorry," said Kate.

"You are not!" said Janet. "And tomorrow, before you go, we have to have a little talk to Officer O'Reilly."

"Now New York," said Martha. "What went on *there*?"

"Ah! Miss Bones!" said Rocky. "I can tell you about her." But he was careful not to say how they met.

"And that fabric Web site you kept visiting?" said Dave.

They set up Viv's laptop at the end of the table and everyone watched in awe as they were given a guided tour of Salamander Imports, which in turn led to Cleverton and Yvette.

"Phew! This would be easier on a whiteboard," said Viv.

"Tell us about Yvette," said Dave.

"Well, actually, we don't know much about her," said Ned. "We didn't have time to talk about ourselves, but I know she's a very good friend."

They made no mention of the Kelp Room.

The phone rang and Dave went to answer it. He returned, looking stunned. "Phew! That was Dekker. I don't know what he means by this but he says the answer to your question, Kate, is 'Definitely yes!' He wants to talk with you kids tomorrow. It seems wildlife was just a sideline for Laana. He was at the heart of the fastest growing little drug-smuggling operation in the west. They've caught his buddy who was an illegal immigrant. And here's one for you, he has a son in Concord prison."

This news was serious and awful.

"Oh my," said Martha with a sharp intake of breath.

"You forget these things," said Dave.

Ned looked at Kate. She had her mouth firmly shut. Rocky caught his eye and slowly raised one eyebrow. They didn't tell about the incident at the prison.

"I think he would only visit his son for some selfish reason," said Ned.

"I bet the son's in prison because of something his father did," said Rocky.

"Nobody knows what goes on in families," said Janet.

"The son might be glad," said Kate with great restraint.

"No sense stewing over it," said Dave. "This is a party, remember? Let's watch Abigail's videos."

Abigail had been taking it all very well for someone consumed with jealousy, so they heaped compliments on her camera work in the Halloween and Starbucks videos. Then with all the talk of street performance, Rocky was made to dance. Rocky's dance to "Alakazar" was a fitting end to the party. He hammed it up doing particular steps for certain states. It was brilliant, and everyone chanted along and laughed till they ached.

"Oh, boy," said Dave, wiping his eyes. "You could make money out of that."

Ned said goodbye to Sneaky, Diabolo and Buckeye, and as a parting gift, the Rockys gave him *The Audubon Guide to the Reptiles of North America*. It was very late when they stepped back over First Stream by flashlight and that night they all slept well.

And next day—*Boof!*— Kate was gone as abruptly as she'd arrived.

Dear Helena,

Kate's cool. She'll be home with you probably tonight. It's Mum I'm writing about. Kate will tell you a hair-raising story and you will wonder about your sister. Well, she's okay.

Before all this, I watched her. She looked fine, but I used to wonder if she was like a broken jar and the pieces were just sitting back in place. But after what we've been through I can tell you there *is* glue between the pieces.

I guess she will always have the cracks, and she'll never be as good as new, but none of us will be.

Thanks for Kate. That sounds stupid, but she's the best cousin I ever had.

And the only one.

Ned

The next goodbye was to the Hunk'o'junk. Janet sold it to the son of one of the mechanics at Acton Motors, who fitted a new exhaust and had it humming like a top in three days. Ned and Janet felt sad, because although the old Chevy had been a trial, it had also been their independence.

"Could have been our coffin."

"Why didn't *we* get it fixed?"

"It was our secret weapon," said Ned.

Going Home

Ja: Where are you Kuza?

Kuza: HOme!

Remote Man: I'll be home soon.

Ja: Are you sad?

Remote Man: Hey, we've got 8 of the top 10 poisonous snakes in the world. How could I stay away? Actually I miss my lizards. Besides, we're getting a new TV!

Sal: """""""""""""BIP BIP BIP BIP BIP"""""""NEWS""""""" Who magazine photo of the wedding of Maria and new husband She is beautiful happy widow, bride of one week and Ready for crazy news? Wedding dress of Maria is SALAMANDER IMPORTS FABRIC!

Kuza: She must have had some left over.

Rocky: Wanted to match the curtains!

Sal: No she uses ALL FOR DRESS and new husband look like Frank except young and more soft

Rocky: She should thank us - Wrote off hubby & supplied wedding dress!!

Ja: How did you get to America, Kuza?

Kuza: Used Laana's credit card. What would Hyacinth say?

Ja: "Dutty water can put out fire" then she would send you straight to church.

Sal: Ho la vache! This is very serious thing

Kuza: Don't you start too

Rocky: She's going to pay back every cent aren't you Kuza

Sal: So— more money news. """"BIP BIP BIP"""""I have good business everyone. Friend lady in Tours shop want to buy Salamander Imports Web site. She like it very much.

Remote Man: Sal, that is GREAT! She can reply to all those customers I ignored.

Rocky: And cover the ISP for the Web site. Didn't tell you but I paid some costs with my savings.

Sal: Rocky I think there will be plenty money. Extra too. We talk later.

Kuza: Sal, you're amaZING! you'll be a millionaire by 16 !!! Hey YOuknow PeepLES we can talkabout A N Y TH ING!!!

Sal: Remote Man. Why that name? You are not cold stand-off person?

Remote Man: Not now. I was

Kuza: Yep, he was

Ja: Rocky, Satday marnin my old friend Lloyd plays guitar in a mento band

Sal: Dance! Rocky I want to see you dance

Rocky: I'm dancing!

Kuza: Now yuh got de riddim mon

Rocky: Dance with me Kuza

Kuza: OOm cha pa cha pa DOOP cha pa cha pa OUCH Rock! You stood on my   FOOT!!!   # % #% %***& #

Ja: No, that was me

Kuza: Wah dat?

Rocky: It was him. Hey, who's the Jamaican?

Remote Man: Salamander?

Sal: Yes I am dancing. See my hair? rainbow

Ja: You makin' me dizzy. I'm floatin' away, dancin' on de tree tops in de marnin' sun.

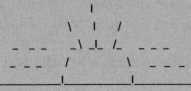

They looked mad, dancing and laughing by themselves as they tapped at the keyboards. Four houses. Two hemispheres. And in the Kingston library, Winifred watched gorgeous Cleverton Lee, his bum wagging as he jigged, bent forward over the computer.

"Nothin' to do with me!" He grinned when he saw her watching him.

Winifred wished she was thirty years younger. "The library is opening in five minutes," she sighed.

For the last time, the sonic boom of the house-brick alarm clock told Ned to get up. Their flight was leaving at ten that night, but there was still packing to be done.

Someone else will be sitting on my seat in that boxy yellow bus. Locker's empty. Got Mr. Nichols' e-mail address, and a few other addresses too. Those girls even made a goodbye cake for my last day. School's not so bad.

Martha had flipped the calender on the kitchen wall to December, so a photogenic raccoon, frozen in the act of raiding a nest, looked down at them eating breakfast.

"The house will be so empty," said Martha, forlorn. "You will always be family now, you know."

Ned, who hardly ever touched anyone, patted her shoulder.

"Chris's coming to stay with us in Australia in April. Why don't you come too?" said Janet.

"Is he, now?" Martha's eyes lit up. "Well, I'll think about that."

"Chris from Tucson? Is Chris a *he*?" said Ned, astonished. "I thought Chris was a *she*."

"He's my son, so I should know," laughed Martha.

"Well then…" was all Ned said, but the two words spoke volumes.

"If you stuck around and paid more attention, you might learn something," laughed Janet.

Then came the ritual Ned had been expecting.

"Hey, Aussie, come here and be measured."

He kicked off his shoes and stood by the door.

"When you arrived, you were as brown and as tough to crack as a Brazil nut.…" Martha peered through her glasses. "Oh *my*! You have *grown*! Janet, he's shot up *two inches*!"

"Anyone would think I was a prize vegetable," grinned Ned.

"You are"—she tapped his head—"and you've grown up here too!"

Then the last goodbye—to Martha at the airport.

"Will you be all right?" she asked Janet.

"I'll be fine. Just ask the Shaker quilt. I can even leave the bed unmade now. You looked after us so well."

They hugged, and Martha blew her nose.

"Time for us to go back to our own trees," said Janet.

At the security check they turned, gave Martha a final wave, and then walked away through the gates.

"Let's go home and see if my McLaren F1 has been delivered."

"We'll walk to Harrison's Knot."

"No more pies."

"I promise you, no more pies."

RM,
YOu won't bELIVE THiS! The python is bAck on the ROCK!
K

DON'T PAT THE WOMBAT!
by Elizabeth Honey

WELCOME TO
GUMBINYA PIONEER CAMP!

School-camp in the Australian bush is everything Mark and
his friends expect and more. There are caves, campfires,
night hikes, wombats, leeches, and mud fights. But best of
all, no homework! Then disaster strikes. Mr. Cromwell
(a.k.a. Crom the Bomb, or simply The Bomb) arrives as
a substitute chaperone. He's the meanest teacher in school,
with one favorite word: detention! The boys are sure their
summer is ruined.

But when The Bomb pushes their friend too far, the
boys take matters into their own hands. . . .

FIDDLEBACK
by Elizabeth Honey

More adventures than you can poke a burnt stick at!

The friends and neighbors of Stella Street have found the perfect camping spot—miles of forest all around, a grassy clearing, a swift-moving stream with a lovely swimming hole. Three moms, three dads, one older neighbor, five kids, and one blissed-out dachshund explore, build campfires, and skinny-dip. It's the kind of magical place where nothing bad could possibly happen.

Well, except for the shady chainsaw-wielding loggers who try to poach some valuable old-growth trees. And the juvenile delinquent who follows the campers from the city and steals their food. And a horrendous storm that washes out the road they drove in on. And the very pregnant mom's chilling announcement: "I think it's time. . . ."

The Stella Street neighbors are in for the time of their lives!